Unforgettable

Also by Paulette Alden

Feeding the Eagles

Crossing the Moon

The Answer to Your Question

Unforgettable

short stories by

Paulette Alden

Unforgettable © 2014 Radiator Press

4900 Washburn Ave. S.
Minneapolis, MN 55410

The author is grateful to the editors of *Ruminator Review*, where "Lost Lake" originally appeared; and to the Minnesota Center for Book Arts, for commissioning "Swimming Snow" as their 1993 Winter Book.

Published in the United States of America

ISBN 978-0-9885189-1-9
First Radiator Press Edition 2014
Library of Congress Control Number: 2013914722

Cover Design by Judy Liautaud/City Creek Press

Radiator Press Logo by Rebecca Swift

Cover Photo credit: Shutterstock/Roman Sigaev

In memory of my mother and father

and for Jeff, again

Contents

The Student

Later, thinking about the student, Miriam couldn't say when she first noticed him. It was early in the term, that she was sure of, maybe even the first class or two, as the anonymous mass of new students, sixteen in this group, began to differentiate into individuals, as she searched, almost unconsciously, for someone to speak to, to speak with, a kindred spirit who would make it all worthwhile. Of course Miriam, being if nothing else democratic, would treat them all alike with an even hand; it was a point of pride that she didn't show favorites. But she had favorites, that much was clear. She would later tell him, when she had driven up from the small liberal arts college in the country where he was her student to Minneapolis, to the big county hospital where he lay near death, that he was her favorite. It was a deathbed scene, though he didn't die. Normally she would never have spoken such a thing, out of fairness to the other students. But weeping all the way into town, a forty-five minute drive, she had lost whatever control she normally had as a teacher; she was reduced to herself, a woman, weeping because he might die. And she had told him, leaning over him a bit in his hospital bed, taking his hand, yellowed with jaundice, with its IV and the wounds on his neck, his wrists, that he, Brian, was her favorite. It seemed incredibly important that he know.

But when did she first notice him? Was it only in retrospect that she would think that he stood out, apart, that he was different in some indefinable way from the other students, bright ones all, but brighter, at least to her? Of course on the surface he was like them, young, twenty years old, an undergraduate at a very good Midwestern college. It might have been that he was particularly interested in writing—she loved those students, the ones who really cared about it the way she did. There were others taking the course who loved writing too. But he, Brian, got in the habit of lingering after class, a particularly interested student who couldn't quite get enough, who wanted to walk with her back from the psychology building, where, oddly, the writing class was held, to the English Department where her office was located. She tried not to show favorites, purposefully not to walk out with him rather than some other student who might want another minute of her time. But they did fall into the habit of walking out together. He had about him a kind of eager quality she found irresistible. He found writing, literature, irresistible, and she sensed too, without actually thinking about it, that he found her irresistible—or was it that she found him irresistible? She did, it was true—irresistible in his youth, his eagerness, his brightness, his happiness.

He was the happiest person she had ever met—was that true? It seemed at times that he literally lit up—she had never quite seen that in anyone else. And he was extremely open, at least with her, beguiling in his guilelessness. He told, at her gentle questioning, for she was curious, how he had grown up all over the West, how his parents had divorced when he was six, how his mother had remarried when he was eight, divorced again, how they had moved every eighteen months or so, from one tract house in some subdivision to another. He seemed such a combination of the absolutely innocent and naive, and also to have a surprisingly mature grasp on things, as if he were old beyond his years. He reminded her of a puppy, somehow—she didn't mean it in a condescending way, but he was that adorable to her, with his blond hair, his bright eyes, the way he'd light up at the sight of her. Late one afternoon about halfway through spring term, when she was walking to her car, far away, across a green field, someone was waving at her, someone was running. It was Brian, on his long, loping legs—he had on shorts and hiking boots—and she could tell from the way he sprinted towards her that he felt pure joy at the sight of her—and she felt the same. Joy. Pure joy.

They might just as well have embraced. But of course they didn't; they walked together to his car, which was closer than hers. It was an incredibly beat-up, huge old Pontiac with multicolored doors, replaced no doubt as they fell off, and painted in crazy colors. He was so proud of it. He had even given it a name, "Mabel."

It brought her great pleasure to see him that day. She often felt lonely at the college. It wasn't just that she was an adjunct, hired part-time and not part of the regular faculty, or that she lived in Minneapolis, forty-five minutes away. It was that everyone was so busy, she herself was so busy and they were all, students and faculty alike, so so busy that she often felt alone. Maybe that was part of why she liked him—he had told her one day in her office of how he felt isolated from others. He was feeling down, and she'd urged him to get some counseling, revealing, as she sometimes did to students whom she sensed needed a little extra nudging in that direction, that she herself had been in therapy at various times (was now), and that it was a great luxury to go in and talk for an hour about oneself. She had laughed a little, lightly. He told her how he had to work twenty to thirty hours at the Subway in town in addition to his student job, along with taking three academic courses at this very demanding school. He had dropped out the previous year—here he alluded to a drinking problem, hard to believe in someone who looked so angelic. He had no time, she discerned, for relaxing, goofing off. He was under pressure, that much she could tell, and he was fragile too, she thought, someone so open, so able to talk about his feelings. He skipped the preliminaries and talked to her directly, as if they were friends.

Later, along with many other questions she would ask herself, Miriam would wonder if the whole class had known that day, before she found out. She liked to think of herself as one who noticed, who paid attention, who was able to *see*—of course all that would come under doubt too—but thinking back, she thought maybe the class was subdued that day; it was hard to say, hard to remember. Whatever the mood, she had carried on, proceeded with the stories under discussion, and it was only after class when two students, Peter and Steve, walked out with her that she learned about Brian.

She had noticed, of course, that he wasn't in class—and he had missed the previous class on Tuesday, which was a bit surprising, because his story was due that day (it was an advanced short story class). It wasn't terribly unusual, though a little, for a student to miss two classes in a row. But what was unusual—she noted it subconsciously as the two students escorted her out—was that they walked her down the hall without speaking. They were both silent, and Miriam fell silent too, without knowing why. It was only when they were outside—it was May, a beautiful spring day after the long Midwestern winter, near the end of the term; the lilacs were in bloom, lots of them, that seems important—that Steve, the smaller, darker, more serious one spoke.

"Have you heard about Brian?"

She was taken by surprise. "No," she said, "I mean, I know he hasn't been in class the last two times."

"He tried to commit suicide," Steve said, and she could feel that he was watching her, delivering the news cautiously and regretfully. He knew she'd care.

"No!" she gasped. "Is he all right?"

Steve was pained and yet eager to tell. The news couldn't be suppressed, it had to burst forth.

"There's a lot of damage to his internal organs. He's not expected to live through the night."

Something in Miriam collapsed. Her body remained standing in the bright daylight, but some part of her—her essence—swooned and fell to the ground. It left her standing there, a hollow shell, maintaining social appearances.

Her mind, left atop the empty shell, struggled to understand. A lot of damage to internal organs? She had an image of him eviscerating himself somehow. She didn't understand.

"He took a massive dose of Tylenol. It destroys the liver ..." and as if he regretted being the one to tell but had to do it, "and he cut himself and tried to hang himself."

Miriam reeled back. She remained standing there, but inside she recoiled in horror. Everything in her cried out to have it not be so, to run the tape backward to the day before, to undo this deed. How could it be? Not Brian! She had never met anyone so happy! Of course he might be more than that—she assumed he was—after all, on the questionnaire she had asked the students to fill out at the beginning of the term, he had written, in response to the final, open-ended question "Tell me something important about yourself," about pain, but in a highly abstract, philosophical manner (he was a philosophy major). And yet, for all that, he could light up with joy like no one she had met.

She thought of the last time she had seen him, a week ago, when he told her the news after class that he had gotten the summer internship for which she had written a letter of recommendation. She had realized, as she was writing the letter, that she didn't know him all that well, or was it that she had some—reservations. It was just that she hoped he would be all right for the job, since she was saying so glowingly that he would be.

He had been so happy about the job that day. She had never seen anyone so happy over so—in a way—little. He was ecstatic. Now everything would fall into place, he exclaimed. Now he was set for the summer. Walking beside her, he had practically bounced. She went along with his enthusiasm, happy for him. She was gratified that she had played a role.

She felt a strong need to get away from Steve and Peter. She thanked them and walked back to her office in an altered state. Everything else had fallen away. She had to get to Minneapolis, she had to get to the hospital, she had to see him. *Don't let him die!* She was not religious, not given to prayer, and it seemed wrong to pray now—cheap, kind of—but maybe this was prayer, this *Don't let him die* chant that had started up in her head, her heart, her whole being. She would cancel office hours—thank goodness she didn't have another class—and drive to Hennepin County Hospital, where Steve and Peter had told her he had been taken by ambulance the previous night. He was too sick, too near death, for the little town hospital. Nothing, she felt, could stop her. It was if she had received news of a family member, she felt that compelled to go to him.

Don't let him die, don't let him die.

The huge county medical center was right in downtown Minneapolis, intimidating in its size and fortress-like facade. Miriam had never had cause to enter it before. She parked in a big, anonymous ramp, the perfect place to get raped and murdered. Normally she was fearful in such ramps, but now she thought that if someone did approach her with rape and murder on his mind, he would find out that his little agenda was sawdust compared to hers. If he caused her one moment's delay, she would strangle the life out of him with her bare hands.

Inside the hospital, she located the information desk. Brian was in intensive care, on the eighth floor, and she took the elevator, feeling intensely focused, as if she were a bullet that had been fired. She didn't know what she would find. At the nurses' station, she explained that she had come to see Brian K … The nurse on duty asked if she was family. "No …" she stammered, "I'm his teacher." "He's around that corner and to the left," the nurse said, waving Miriam in that direction.

Miriam hesitated. She hadn't really expected to be admitted so easily, to be able to see him. Her heart beat hard as she went down the hall. There on a hospital bed in the hall lay Brian, breathing, asleep, alive, a sheet pulled up to his chest. He wasn't even in a room, just an open, indeterminate space, all by himself. Miriam crept up to him and looked into his face. He was so young! *Like the Pieta, the beautiful sad body of Jesus in Mary's arms.* She had never seen him so close, never stared at his face like this before. She drank him in, even as she felt she shouldn't; a face was private, she was violating his privacy by looking at him when he was unaware. Scraggly whiskers sprouted from his chin, touching in their blond sparseness. He looked poised at some halfway point between boy and man, as if he could tip either way. There was a yellow tint to him— the failing liver. But he was breathing, he was alive! Miriam felt like weeping again. He couldn't die. The thought of it was like a rip through her whole self. Her own life, she realized, would be permanently rent if he died. He was so young, there was so much ahead of him, he didn't even know … He had tried to kill himself. How could he try to destroy what she herself valued so much—loved, even? It didn't seem possible. The whole thing had a nightmare feel.

She pulled up a little plastic chair nearby and sat by his bed, keeping watch. It surprised her that no one else was around. Of course there was no family in town, they'd have been called, they'd be coming, she assumed. How must his mother feel, what must she be going through? Miriam put her head in her hands and supported its surprising weight. Probably the staff wouldn't let in any of his friends, the other students. But they let her in, his teacher. *Oh, why couldn't she have saved him?* She watched his chest rise and fall, and she had never been so thankful for anything in her life. She couldn't bear that he die this young, that he die by his own hand. There was a rope burn around his neck where he had tried to hang himself—someone had spread a greasy ointment like Vaseline on it. And his wrists were bandaged. He had tried so hard to kill himself! It must have taken place over time—not some spontaneous decision, but several attempts, hours of trying. She knew, instinctively, how he would have felt like a failure as he failed to die, that he couldn't even do this one thing right. The weeping rose in her again. Oh Brian! He was stirring, waking up.

She stood beside him. He was coming to. He opened his eyes. His hands were folded one atop the other on his chest, and she put her own hand on his. She felt his warm, yellow skin, shocked that she had actually touched him. He looked up and saw her. "Miriam!" he spoke her name and his eyes lit up, the old joy at the sight of her. He had called her by her first name from the start, not Ms. Batson or Professor Batson, as most students did. "I came as soon as I heard," she said. "They let me see you because I'm your teacher." She was looking into his face, his eyes, drinking him in. She had expected someone so near death to be groggy, but he was perfectly alert, totally clear, she saw. She didn't know what to say. "I missed you in class today," she tried, smiling into his eyes. "That's two missed classes in a row, you know," and she raised her eyebrows in mock warning, a takeoff on the role of stern professor. "I'm sorry," he said seriously, missing the joke, piercing her heart. He was always so quick to apologize, to accept blame, to want to please. "Oh God, Brian," she said. "I wish I had known. I wish you had called me or I had called you when you weren't there on Tuesday. I didn't realize!"

"It all just caught up with me," he said. "I'd gotten so behind in everything, I didn't see another way out." He paused for a moment. "Would you do me a favor? Call Margo at YouthWorks and tell her she can hire someone else for this summer if she needs to, in light of what's happened?" She nodded her head. She kept her hand on his. "I'll return those two books I borrowed from you," he said. "All the time I was trying to kill myself, I was worried about how you'd get your books back."

"Oh Brian. It's all right, don't worry about it, it doesn't matter." And then, because it felt so urgent that he know, that she tell him, she said, "You're my favorite, you know." His eyes widened in a kind of exhausted surprise. For a long moment they both absorbed this news in silence. Then with his thumb, very delicately, he stroked the top of her hand where it rested on his hand. They hung there in that moment. Miriam stared down at their hands, mesmerized by his thumb, which she'd never looked at before—how masculine it was, but also still slender in its youth, slightly stubby with the nail cut too close. She wanted to cry her heart out—*you're alive, alive!* That seemed the most important thing, the only thing. "I'm so glad you're alive," she said finally, when she could stand it no more. He nodded his head and shut his eyes. "I wish I was dead," he said.

Miriam was not unacquainted with depression. And not just from the literature, as they say. She knew what it felt like to want to die, or maybe more precisely in her case, to want not to be alive. She had had those moments. Who hasn't? But she saw that on the continuum of despair, Brian had traveled much farther than she ever had, and it shocked her. It bewildered her. He was not out of the woods yet, she learned from the little crowd of students who had gathered in the intensive-care waiting room. The next twenty-four hours would tell. His liver, struggling. Not out of the woods yet—where did that expression come from? Those woods frightened her—how dark and deep they seemed, how lost one would be in them. Then there was the fact that he didn't want to live. She had assumed, naively she now saw, that he'd be as happy to be alive as she was that he lived. But he still wanted to die.

She sat with the students, listening to them. Some were from the college and six or seven were high school students. Immediately Miriam knew, seeing them, especially the high school students, that they were into drugs. They looked normal enough, they weren't punked out with orange, spiked hair and multiple body piercings, but there was about them an air of secret, clandestine lives, a facade of passing that didn't quite obscure the sense that all was not as it seemed. She bet they lied to their parents and were home as little as possible.

The college students were harder to peg. They were

typical of the students at the college, unusually bright, good-looking kids, each one accustomed to succeeding, standing out, taking oneself seriously as a Self. One, a handsome/pretty young man, introduced himself to her as Matthew, and made a point of telling her that he was not just a friend of Brian's. What did he mean? Miriam inferred some sort of sexual relationship, though she hadn't imagined that Brian was gay or bisexual. But of course that age was given to sexual experimentation, confusion, ambiguity. It was sort of cool at the college to be bisexual, and Brian was very attractive physically, with his bright good looks, his boyish energy, his mixture of innocence and experience.

The chaplain of the college arrived with a woman whom she introduced as Brian's mother, Karen, and an older woman, Barb, his grandmother. They had just arrived from Tennessee, had been in to see Brian, and now wanted to say a few words to the waiting students. Miriam introduced herself, explained her role as Brian's teacher. "Oh, I've heard about you from Brian!" Karen exclaimed, reaching out for Miriam, who embraced her. Karen was about Miriam's own age, maybe a few years older, though it was hard to say. Miriam saw that Karen lived a different life from herself. Miriam hadn't had children, she fancied herself a writer, she taught in college, she had a thin veneer of sophistication, whereas Karen was just folks, part of the real world, a divorced, somewhat overweight, middle-aged woman in a pants suit, someone without pretension and not many options. Miriam shook the hand of the grandmother, a woman in her seventies, still vital and weathered into a kind of tempered steel. She was wearing a royal-blue sweat suit and Nikes, sensible traveling clothes, Miriam noted.

Karen made a little speech to the waiting students, thanking them for their support. She referred to God several times. She seemed to know what to do, what to say, how to act. Miriam was impressed. How did people shift gears so quickly to rise to the occasion? Yesterday, for all Karen knew, her son was doing fine, and now he was lying in intensive care, having tried to kill himself. How had she felt, getting the phone call, having to get on a plane and fly here, not knowing if Brian would be dead or alive when she arrived? Miriam could hardly stand it. She had missed out on motherhood herself, and maybe it was just as well, she often thought. She didn't have the guts for it.

That night Miriam and her husband Ted went to a neighborhood restaurant, moderately expensive with white tablecloths and stylish food. There were several items on the menu that Miriam could not pronounce. They came here often, especially when they needed relatively easy respite. Miriam ordered the lamb shank because it came with mashed potatoes. Comfort food, and Miriam needed comforting.

She told Ted the tale of getting the news, of her mad dash to Minneapolis, of spending the afternoon at the hospital, meeting the students and Brian's mother and grandmother—the life-and-death drama of it all. Ted listened with interest, but he didn't know Brian, and after a while they moved on to other things, a relief in a way. Miriam felt that she couldn't really convey the intensity of her feelings about what had happened, nor was she sure she would want to. She hardly understood it herself. She was aware that if another of her students had tried to commit suicide, she would have been shocked, saddened, but she wouldn't have responded as she did to Brian. She was surprised at herself. All her usual reserve, considerable, had crumbled.

She didn't tell Ted that she had told Brian that he was her favorite. That seemed too personal, something she was still absorbing herself. But every now and then, over dinner, she'd trace again in her mind that moment when she had told him, and how he had stroked her hand lightly with his thumb.

Remembering that moment, she felt a kind of thrill and wondered if she was in love with Brian. She accepted that one could be in love, by degrees and in various ways, with many people and never even have to realize it too consciously. What did it mean, anyway, to be in love with someone? There was chemistry, certainly. Had there been something sexual in the way their hands met, in that surprising touch? Sexual seemed the least of it, however—off the mark, too simplistic, missing the point. It had been so intimate, that was it, as if for that moment they had touched … She didn't believe in souls, exactly, she shied away from the term, especially in writing. Whenever a student used it—a not infrequent occurrence—she'd write in the margin, "not sure," or if she felt like it, simply "no." "Soul" was so overused, so hackneyed, really. Miriam turned up her nose at it, thinking it too imprecise, vague, easy, really. "Our souls touched." The stuff of romance writers. But she had felt, for that moment in the hospital, that she and Brian had touched if not souls exactly, then selves, their true selves, outside all the normal boundaries, rules, and roles. They had touched. *Touched.* It was not something she would ever talk about to anyone else, even Ted, to whom she told most everything. Because to try to describe it, to explain it, would kill it, destroy it, like trying to catch a bubble. Pop.

She and Ted had been married for—what, now? Thirteen years. A long time, also short. Miriam had been twenty-nine when they met, Ted twenty-six. They had lived together, wary in a way and in no hurry, for four years before they wed. Miriam looked back on those young people they had once been as though they were like her current students, fledglings whom she viewed with affection and hope, aware of how far they had to go, how much they needed to learn. In their wedding pictures (they had been married in a civil ceremony at the courthouse, downplaying the whole thing), their faces looked surprisingly innocent to her now, especially Ted's, who was almost baby-faced then. He had just finished law school, Miriam was writing, and they hadn't thought of themselves as particularly green, but now Miriam knew they had been. Now here they were, middle-aged or at least solidly on the cusp, a number of things behind them, a lot of options closed, choices made, possibilities squandered. They were well into the realm of consequences.

Did they ever touch? Certainly they did, usually on Sunday mornings, their own private service. But did they ever really break through all the layers of habit, familiarity, routine and comfort, actually, to really *touch*? Miriam thought of the finger of God reaching out to Adam's in the Sistine Chapel, that electric connection, that intimacy. Maybe that was only possible when things were new, or in a life-or-death situation. It wasn't that the thrill, exactly, was gone, it was just that it got buried under so much stuff, the stuff of a life together. Miriam knew she was loved. She found this both expected and extraordinary. She understood that at the end of her life, she would know with complete certainty that she had been loved—deeply, truly, fully. It was incredible, really, to be so loved. Ted told her all the time, "I love you. I can't believe how much I love you." And she loved Ted. Love permeated their lives. Love familiar, known, experienced, cherished. But it was no longer new.

Miriam remembered when love was new, brand new. Not with Ted—she was too old at twenty-nine when she met him for love to be new, but new when she was twenty herself, and he wasn't even her first lover, she had had sex before him, but he was her first love. She'd had boyfriends, crushes, flings, but she loved this boy, this young man, Tom. She had felt incredibly happy in his presence, sure of herself, strong and right. It had been spring then, too.

Another May day, in Chapel Hill, where she was a senior in college. Her Russian literature class, the desk chairs with their worn patina of wood scattered around the classroom. Before class, the windows open, the smell of spring in the air, and a young man asking her if he could borrow her *Daily Tarheel*. She looks at him, at his brown eyes with gold in them, and later, when they're lying in bed, she'll see that there are golden freckles under his eyes. He will always be to her some lovely blend of brown and gold. He has a full shock of dark brown hair, rich and warm, burnished somehow, she likes his looks, looks forward to seeing him in their next class, and she senses with certainty that he is interested in her, the borrowing of the newspaper just a ploy. He asks to borrow it again the next class, and she's ready, she's on to him, there is that delicious subtext, they know what's going on, where this will lead, and it *is* delicious, because you can't be sure, after all; she thinks she knows, but maybe she's wrong, maybe it's not what she thinks at all. It is as delectable as running into the ocean, the shock and thrill of it all, and then lying on the warm sand beach, the way she will lie in his warm arms before too long.

They become lovers, and she loves him. She loves his golden brown eyes, the golden brown freckles, his auburn hair with its glints of gold, and his golden warm voice, like syrup. She likes his humor, his lilting laugh, his golden warmth in the way he loves her. He seems to see her the way she's always wanted to be seen, known, the way she knows herself to be, now that he has shown her.

Another spring day. She's walking toward campus in the bright, beautiful morning down the street where she rents an apartment in the top of an old house on Stevens Street. And there he is, Tom, at the other end of the street, walking toward her to meet her. They don't run toward one another and embrace, like lovers in a cigarette commercial or a French film. They walk slowly and deliberately toward one another, looking at one another, smiling with a perfect understanding. This is the most perfect moment of her life, Miriam will sometimes think. She plays it over and over in her head, relishing the feeling of that moment when she saw that he had come to meet her, and how they walked towards one another, looking one another in the eye. She had felt joy. Pure joy.

It ended, eventually, as those things tend to do. It didn't even last that long—several months, though it felt like a lifetime. And then she was going away to graduate school, and he still had a year left at college, but it wasn't that. It was—what? He stopped loving her, was what it came down to. Not that he ever betrayed her or was in any way cruel to her, but he cooled off, he lost interest, he moved on. It had run its course, was all. Though it took her years to get over it, being the way she was. And after that, she wasn't young in the same way any more. It wasn't a matter of blame. She had to grown up sometime. She couldn't be an innocent forever, someone had to break her heart, it was inevitable, she was aching for it, the natural thing. But too bad, really, that some parts of us have to die. They die, they're killed, we kill them, they're gone, but don't they live in us still? Some little vestigial heart of them, still?

Miriam called the nurses' station the first thing in the morning to hear how Brian had fared overnight. She'd spent a tortured night full of strange, nightmarish dreams, fearing he had taken a turn for the worst, fearing he might die. Having seen him the previous day, she didn't believe that he would die. But then why had they said at the hospital that the next twenty-four hours were crucial? She didn't know a thing about the liver, about how the body could fail. She didn't know much about anything, she realized, even though she called herself a teacher.

The nurse on duty said Brian was still in critical condition, but his pulse and blood pressure were better. He was on oxygen because he had developed some congestion during the night, and they didn't want him to develop pneumonia. When Miriam went over to the hospital in the afternoon, she learned from Karen that Brian was out of danger, beyond the immediate crisis. But he was still severely depressed. Mostly he slept, exhausted from the events of the past few days. Occasionally his mother or grandmother would go in to see him, and once Miriam did, but he was asleep, so she didn't wake him.

It was the weekend, and Miriam went about her life on one level, but on another level, a deeper level, she was preoccupied with Brian, mourning him in a way. So there *had* been a death of sorts, after all. She found herself wanting to be alone and she was glad when Ted had to go into the office on Saturday. She was free to talk to Brian in her mind. There was a lot she wanted to say to him, but it wasn't on the level of conversation. In real life, in person, what would come out would be awkward attempts at communication. What she longed for, what she could only have when she was by herself, was some deep and meaningful dialogue from the heart. Because a lot was in her heart. It didn't seem appropriate to put it into words, so intense and personal it was, so urgent and necessary, like prayer.

On Tuesday, Miriam had to return to teaching her two classes at the college. She had been at the hospital a lot over the weekend; she couldn't seem to stay away. She had seen Brian a couple of times, but each time he was so sleepy that she just stayed a few moments. He had insomnia; his sleep schedule was reversed. Miriam felt like shouting at someone (who?), "Just get him on a regular cycle so he sleeps at night and is awake during the day!" But of course it wasn't as simple as that.

She informed the students in Brian's class of how he was, and they absorbed the news somberly, but then they all moved on to the coursework of the day. When she walked around campus she felt a strange absence, knowing that she would not see Brian. It made her sad to think that he wouldn't be coming back, that things couldn't go back to the way they had been, or appeared to be. Karen had said he wouldn't be returning to the college. She was taking him home to get him away from bad influences, give him a fresh start. Miriam looked up his address in the student directory and drove by the house where he had rented the room, where he had nearly died. It was a shabby, run-down affair, beyond the typical student housing in its disrepair. But Brian wouldn't have cared about that. He would have been happy to be off campus and independent. Until things caught up with him. All around the house, the lilacs were blooming their hearts out. There was no sign of "Mabel." Karen had said they were selling the car.

When Miriam got back to Minneapolis that afternoon, she went by the hospital to see Brian. She had collected some books from her office that he might like and had bought him a journal and some pens.

She found him sitting in a chair in his hospital room in his hospital gown and robe. His body, it seemed, was making a miraculous recovery. His liver had regenerated, something that could happen in the young. He seemed very up, exuberant in the way he used to be. He leaped up when he saw her, he seemed about to embrace her, he was so happy to see her. "I feel like I've come back," he said to her. "I realized I was going to live, so okay!" He smiled his beautiful smile.

It all sounded so convincing, honest and true. But Miriam didn't trust it; she'd been burned before. He still seemed so fragile, so at risk. She knew the world was going to be a tough place for Brian. She had so much she wanted to say to him, to try to tell him, to teach him, but she held her tongue. She wanted to say she knew a lot of grieving and healing would have to go on with him, but maybe now wasn't the time; he wasn't strong enough, he seemed so happy ... What she really wanted to do was hold his hand. She was surprised at the intensity of this desire. To hold his hand, not to speak, but to be in communion with him in that way. What she felt was beyond words. She thought again of that moment when she had placed her hand on his, of how they had touched. Everything was being said then that needed to be said, only through their hands. But she couldn't imagine taking his hand now.

She stood to go. Brian walked her to the door. They paused there for a moment to say goodbye. She felt that they weren't exactly these two separate bodies, these two awkward people standing there, a twenty-year-old student and his forty-six-year-old teacher, but two old—*that word*—souls, two selves, outside of time and place. He was taller than she was, and slender like a boy. She felt like leaning against him to draw comfort from his beating heart. Again she felt the impulse to take his hand, but it seemed too strange, inappropriate, she wasn't sure what it meant or that he'd understand. And, she reminded herself, he's just a kid, and a pretty messed-up one, at that. Maybe he was both, a temporal being and an eternal one. Maybe he saw that she was, too.

He couldn't sleep at night and so he would read. Miriam loved how he loved reading, how excited he got about literature. He thought Miriam's book of short stories, which she had given him, was fantastic, but that the first story was too disjointed. He was sharp. Miriam encouraged him to write his childhood memories in the journal she had given him. His psychiatrist at the hospital had told him he was good at intellectualizing, but had trouble with his feelings (Did they all say that?). He couldn't sleep, he had insomnia, a lot on his mind. And Miriam would wake up at night too, too, three o'clock, four o'clock, thinking about him. She would carry on long conversations with him, earnest, intense lessons she wanted to teach him. She thought of other students she had taught, and realized that she had loved a lot of them. She had loved them and raised them during the term, and she had tried to teach them, not just the subject of the course and certainly not anything about how to be, to live—she hardly knew herself—but she had held them in her heart somehow. That was the best she could describe it. For awhile, they had been hers, and then she let them go. That was the natural order of things. But in Brian's case, the natural order had been broken.

She went over to the hospital nearly every day. He was in a psych ward now, and one day she found him at a table in his robe and pajamas, still with a yellow glow to him, though his liver was recuperating well. He had his books and journal there on the table, and he was taking some psychological test that he put aside when she sat down.

"I'm going to start electroshock therapy on Wednesday," he said. "We saw this film. It isn't like *One Flew Over the Cuckoo's Nest*. The thing is, I'm feeling good and don't think I need it. But they say the depression will cycle back up. So they hope the electroshock will knock it out. I can't take drugs yet, because of my liver. I may have some memory loss from the shock treatment, but nothing major."

Miriam nodded her head. She hated to think of it, to think of him, Brian, getting jolted in his head, some of his memory being blown out, any part of him being destroyed. *Don't forget me*, she thought.

"I guess I'll be going back to Tennessee after the treatments," he said. "That's what Mom wants me to do. She's afraid to leave me up here by myself. I don't really want to go back to the college. Too many bad associations." He was rubbing lotion on his arms where the jaundice made him itch.

"What do you think you'll do?"

"Maybe get a job as a waiter for awhile. I might try a gay bar, because I'd get better tips." He laughed slyly. "I can't drink for six months, the doctors say. No alcohol or drugs."

"You know," Miriam said suddenly, "you might be able to stay with us a little while after you get out of the hospital. Have a little vacation, in a way, before you get on with your life."

A vision formed in her mind, of Brian in their guest room, a clean, quiet place. She'd take care of him, fix him good meals, he'd relax in the backyard, walk around the lake, sleep through the night, and grow well. She'd look after him and he'd be okay. She'd make sure.

"That's really nice of you," he said. "I do think I'll stick around for this concert that's going to be in town on June 11, Lollapalooza. Do you know about it?"

Miriam thought she had heard of it, but she didn't know much about rock concerts. Too old, too out of it.

"Won't there be a lot of drinking and drugs there?" she asked.

"Not for me," Brian laughed.

"Are you sure you can handle it? I mean, being around a lot of using like that?"

"It's true I like to party," he said, "and I've been pretty wild in the past. You know, I used to get high to read the stories for your class, and then I could see several levels of meaning in them."

"Oh Brian!" Miriam exclaimed. "Don't you know you'll mess up your fabulous mind?"

"I choose to do them," he said. "I have this desire to experience heightened states of consciousness. But I'm in control of that decision. I want to eventually try them all, but only when I can handle them."

"Really, Brian. You seem so at risk without even realizing it."

"It's just that I feel so well now. It's so different from when I was depressed. I actually feel better and happier sober than I did when I was high." He was talking a little fast, animatedly. "I've been into drugs pretty heavy. When I had marijuana around, I smoked it all the time. I've even dealt drugs, LSD and marijuana."

Miriam wanted to put her hands over her ears.

"I still want to go further with LSD. That's one experience I want to pursue. I know people who see different realities and I want to experience that."

"Brian, you sound chemically dependent."

"No!" he said emphatically. "Drugs are something I choose. I never did any stuff because I had to. It was always a choice. Even when I abused them, it was my choice."

"But why would you choose to do that!" Miriam said. She felt a kind of despair rise in her. "To abuse …"

Brian didn't answer.

"I don't understand that at all," Miriam said, shaking her head.

"Well, I do worry that maybe it might do a number on my memory later. I met this woman in group here who has memory problems from using LSD twenty years ago."

"We're talking about your whole life here," Miriam said, "the rest of it, how you can blow it. I don't want you to blow it."

"I don't either," he said softly.

"Our minister back home knows an educational psychologist we think would be the perfect mentor for Brian," Karen was saying. She and Miriam were having a cup of coffee in the hospital cafe. "Brian's searching for some religious guidance—for Christian faith."

It was true that Brian was searching for something. Developing his spiritual side might actually be the answer, if there were any answers. Miriam imagined him going back to Tennessee, being "saved," even born again, mouthing horrible platitudes about putting his life in God's hands. But even as she was thinking this, even as she nodded and smiled into Karen's earnest face, Miriam knew she was being both a snob and an ignoramus. She had been raised

Southern Baptist herself, but had come to see convention-
al religious beliefs as sophistry, something simple-minded
people used to console themselves, a form of denial regarding the way things really were. Heaven was for soft-
ies, for people who couldn't take it. Even as she thought
these thoughts, Miriam knew they were foolish, shallow.
Without even realizing when it had happened, she'd become the worst kind of skeptic.

Brian was reading C.S. Lewis's *The Screwtape Letters*. Miriam hadn't read any religious thinkers since her
twenties. She had taken a Religions of the World course in
college and been attracted by the readings. She had even,
when she was young, imagined that she'd grow up to be
a missionary. The options for women in the early sixties,
when she was thirteen, fourteen, fifteen, had seemed so
limited: wife, of course, but if that didn't work out, teacher or nurse and for a select few, missionary. There were
women missionaries, Miriam knew, which meant you
could be true to your gender, i.e., good, self-sacrificing,
and still have some adventure in your life. Travel to Af-
rica, that sort of thing. There was something appealing
in the image of a spinster wearing ugly oxford shoes and
plain dark clothes, ministering to sick, unsaved Africans.
She had also, briefly, during her adolescence, in the small
window of time before she actually got it that she was female and all that implied, imagined becoming a preacher.
Not that she knew any women preachers. But the idea
of preaching, standing up in public and talking to people
about the really important things—the state of one's soul,
one's relationship to God, the eternal, even—had stirred
her. She had been drawn to it mightily.

She had become a writer instead. It hadn't been an
accident; it was actually the right thing for her. Still, she
admired, even envied, spiritual people. She understood,
at least at moments, that there was more than she could

grasp, an underlying order and meaning. This suicide attempt of Brian's had raised a lot of questions. She tried to sort it out, to make some sense of it. She believed, for starters, that clinical depression, such as Brian had, was biologically based. Chemicals were messed up in his brain.

But she also believed it was a disease, in some sense, of the soul, at least in Brian's case. She felt in him a tremendous battle going on, between good and evil, the devil and God, if you will, his corporal and spiritual self. She was surprised to find herself interpreting along these Old Testament lines. But it seemed to her that he was struggling to decide which way he'd go, who he'd become. She felt in him such a spiritual side and then, at other moments, he just seemed an immature, self-absorbed kid who wanted to do drugs, regardless of what it cost him and his family and friends. This idea of staying on for the Lollapalooza concert confounded her. After all he had been through— and put others through—why would he make the decision to stay on in Minnesota and go to this rock concert? She understood it meant a lot to him, he wanted to be there, see the scene. But in light of having almost killed himself, it seemed a frivolous, somewhat foolhardy desire. Why take the chance? Why put himself in temptation's way? Did she almost say "the Devil's way?" But when she had asked him about it, what he said had made sense. He didn't want to become a "cripple," as he put it, after this suicide attempt. He felt it was important for him to prove that he could handle it. It would be a way of bringing this phase of his life to closure—to say goodbye to people.

It made sense. He sounded so reasonable. He was so serious and thoughtful that she had to take him seriously. She respected him, even though she wanted to dismiss him. She felt his youth, his openness and honesty, his striving to have an authentic self. But another side of her feared he was chemically dependent. He might talk a good talk, and he did, but Miriam was afraid of drugs. She didn't believe he could control his desire for them. She had never wanted, herself, to experience other realities through chemicals. Reality as she knew it was plenty to deal with.

Brian could get out of the hospital on passes now, and so Miriam invited him over for dinner one night. She bought some nice porterhouse steaks, potato salad, and butter-leaf lettuce for a salad, and that morning she made a banana cake, singing to herself as she stirred and baked. She picked him up at his C2 ward at the hospital at five o'clock. The staff person on duty shook Miriam's hand, said he wanted to meet Brian's teacher. He went to get Brian, who had just showered. He came bounding out, his hair still wet, obviously excited and eager. He seemed a little hyper and maybe nervous, a bit high-strung. He hugged Miriam, which surprised her. She got the feeling he had thought about it and decided it was okay to hug her. He was touching to her in his youth, his masculine assertiveness, which seemed a little green, tender. She felt like a girl around him, a bit flustered herself, and yet she also knew herself to be his teacher, somehow responsible for his well-being.

At the house he sat in the backyard talking to Ted while she worked in the kitchen, icing the banana cake, making the salad. It was a beautiful evening—just what she had wanted. Out the window she could see Brian's feet in his white Nikes, big like a puppy's, where he was stretched out in the chaise lounge. She heard the murmur of his and Ted's voices. She had a feeling of great peace and comfort; at least for the moment, all was well. What would it have been like to have a son, to have him home from college? She thought how much she wanted to treat Brian, to give him this beautiful evening, to feed him. Ted grilled the steaks, and Brian ate his down to the bone, really enjoying it, while Miriam watched, feeling happy—the guy seemed starved! He reminded her of the baby birds she had tried to save when she was little, until you learn you can't.

He thanked Miriam several times for the dinner as she drove him back to the hospital. He always had such manners, such a sense of appreciation and gratitude. She dropped him off outside the psych ward. He had complete freedom to come and go now. But even as Miriam watched him walk away, she couldn't help wondering if he would indeed go back to his room. She couldn't help thinking that he might kill himself. He might just walk off into the night and die.

Monday. Brian had been over for dinner on Thursday. When she took him back to the hospital that night, she had asked him to call her next week, they'd get together, she'd have time. She hadn't heard from him since. It was only Monday, but Miriam felt the same way she used to feel when she was waiting for a man to call. Waiting and waiting. Obsessed, really, she noted with bemusement. What was going on over there at the hospital? She was still anxious at some level that he wasn't okay, that he'd try to kill himself again. But she also knew it wasn't that. Again she thought of that moment when they touched, when something passed between them. She knew she should back off, begin to let go, but her mind was preoccupied with him, with wanting him to call. It puzzled her. She hadn't realized that she was still susceptible to these feelings, fantasies even. She would never cross a line with him, but some deep part of her wished that they could just exist outside of time, outside of their real lives.

She wondered what it would be like to go to bed with him. How young he would be, how excited, and she would be the older, more experienced woman, the teacher. This in some world outside of all the messy details, the fact that he was suicidal, fragile, vulnerable, twenty, and she, married. She felt ashamed of herself for such a fantasy. What would Ted think? It would hurt him, and what would Karen, Brian's mother, think, for God's sake? Miriam shook her head to try to clear it. It was only a fantasy, she told herself, *no one will ever have to know.* In the fantasy she was not exactly herself, not her temporal self exactly, but some eternal self. In actual time, she felt she was growing older—she was almost middle-aged, she was losing her sex appeal. She had heard that in menopause, a woman's lips get thinner. The world looked on her, she felt, as a nice married lady, but didn't give her a second glance. She felt intuitively that Brian did notice. But then he was at that age, he noticed anything in a skirt. He radiated sexual interest, pheromones, and Miriam was responding to that, she supposed. Maybe those invisible airborne molecules were just wafting around him all the time, and she had got a snootful.

It was Wednesday before he called. Miriam noted that was good, that he was showing good judgment, really, if he even thought about any of this. He was more appropriate than she was! It occurred to her that he wasn't obsessed with her the way she was with him. But then she hadn't tried to kill herself! Now he had a life to resume, friends his own age, and a heck of a future to figure out. It was right that Miriam be a piece of that future, but only a small piece. She began to think about when he would leave Minneapolis, return to Tennessee, and what a relief that would be for her.

• • •

The Lollapalooza concert was on Saturday night. He'd be getting out of the hospital on Friday, staying with friends in St. Paul for the concert, and then he'd be leaving on Tuesday. He'd had his airline ticket sent to Miriam, and she would bring it to him when they got together on Monday to say goodbye.

Miriam bought a new black bra for the occasion. Not that she had any intention of Brian seeing it. It was just that he had stirred something in her, some desire to be desirable, to be available again. To be young again. She no longer knew if she was a good-looking woman (had she ever been?). Ted said she was, but he had to, didn't he?

Lollapalooza. What did the word even mean? Miriam didn't know. Maybe it was just an expression of a mood, a feeling, a generation. X? Alternative rock, whatever that meant. Miriam had read about it in the newspaper: "spring break for the alienated." Nine hours of music with a main stage and second stage, with a bazaar of ethnic food and clothing. It sounded fun, if you were twenty years old. Bands like Primus, Alice in Chains, Dinosaur Jr., and Arrested Development (of all things). Brian had loaned Miriam an Alice in Chains CD, trying to educate her regarding his music. Who was the student now? The music was strange, black, heavy, hopeless. She couldn't listen to it for long.

She tried not to think too much about the concert over the weekend. It was in God's hands, even though she didn't believe in God. At least it was out of her hands. Maybe Brian was right to go. He had the right instincts, to be who he was, to do what you do when you're twenty years old. He was certainly no fool. But Miriam wasn't sure which part of him would win out. She felt as if she were holding her breath, even as she went about her business.

Waiting. Waiting and waiting. Not just waiting to hear

about Lollapalooza—though she was waiting for that—but other waiting, waiting specific and vague. Specifically, she was waiting to hear if her new book, a memoir, would be accepted by a certain New York publisher. It had been there over five months now. Waiting. There had been an exciting break in the waiting when the editor called out of the blue two months ago to say she had just begun to read the manuscript and "loved it." Then nothing. Nothing, that is, except waiting. It put Miriam's nerves on edge.

Waiting was underestimated as a human scourge. She recalled reading a line somewhere, "most of life is waiting." How true. She felt she was always waiting, that life was not really happening yet, but would when the waiting was over. It never was. She admired people who gathered no moss. She was not one of them. Her own tendency was towards caution and conservatism. Lollapalooza indeed.

Being a writer consisted so much of waiting, isolation, and boredom. Or was that only Miriam? She tried to set up the conditions for writing that she thought she needed: time, solitude, introspection. Then she was bored, lonely, and depressed. It was hard, day in and day out, year in and year out, to pull fresh material out of her imagination and memory. Most of the time, what she had to say seemed predictable and stale. But occasionally something would burst forth—something rich, funny, sad, alive—out of all that deadness. It was unpredictable. She thought sometimes that the very deadness, the waiting, were necessary for the alive thing to burst forth. But she paid a price.

Waiting, boredom, depression. All the fun things! Often her soul felt—to borrow Joyce Carol Oates's description—as flat as a playing card. When did Joyce Carol Oates have time to feel that way? She was so busy bursting forth with books all the time. Miriam could tell her a thing or two about flat souls. How did life get so circumscribed? A long marriage, middle age, life itself. You worked so hard to be secure, mature, safe, out of crisis, and then you die of boredom. Hard to get it right. She wished she could "do" something: burst out, run away, have an affair. Commit suicide? That would be dramatic, and humans needed drama. Maybe she was having withdrawal from Brian's suicide attack. It had been like a drug.

He didn't drink or do drugs at Lollapalooza. He hadn't even had that great a time, it seemed, maybe because he couldn't use. He had said goodbye to his friends and realized, in a way, how little there was there.

He and Miriam were talking on the phone Sunday night, making plans to get together Monday for one last time before he'd fly home to Tennessee on Tuesday.

Monday dawned hot and humid. Summer had arrived, as full-blown as the sudden leaves on the trees. Miriam dressed in a sleeveless blouse and a skirt with birds on the material, and underneath, her own little secret, the new black bra. She felt sexy and it was great. Great! She hadn't died yet.

She picked him up at his friends' apartment, a brownstone on Grand Avenue in St. Paul around one o'clock. He seemed in bad shape to her—bleary-eyed, washed-out looking—but of course he had stayed up most of the night of the concert.

Miriam saw that he was growing a little beard, like a goatee. It looked a little ridiculous, as if he couldn't quite pull off having a beard. Yet it did change his looks, made him different somehow, and for Miriam it broke the spell. He was no longer the boy he had been when she knew him in the spring, when the lilacs were in bloom.

Brian was excited because he was going to see his ex-girlfriend Sam—short for Samantha—that night.

"Maybe I'll get laid," he said gleefully, and Miriam laughed.

"So tell me about you and Sam," she said.

"We were deeply in love for a while," Brian said. He gave a tremendous yawn. Miriam wondered if he was really awake yet. "But I didn't want to go steady over the summer—this was last summer—and she ended up falling in love with someone else, an older guy, like thirty-five. I'd really like to sleep with her again, mainly to get laid. Not that I don't like her and am not attracted to her and all that—but ... "

Good, Miriam thought. It's good he's horny, a good sign. Horny is the opposite of depressed.

"I don't really like to play the field," he confided. "I like to be in love." And again he yawned.

"Do you need a nap?" Miriam asked.

"Oh, I think I'll revive around Sam," he said, and Miriam had to laugh again. *She* in her secret black bra wasn't too stimulating, but Sam would be. Just as it should be. Well, Ted would be the beneficiary.

Miriam took him to a restaurant for a late lunch, her last chance to feed him. He had a psychiatrist appointment at three. She noted that she was glad there were some time limits. She had errands to run this afternoon, things to do. This particular waiting—this watch—was done.

She double-parked outside the main entrance of the hospital. "You know," he said, "the doctors here still marvel over me. 'The miracle person' they call me, because I survived such a serious suicide attempt." Miriam nodded. For once there were no words in her mind, nothing left to say. She reached over to embrace him, to say goodbye.

She held his warm alive body, his warm alive self. Then she let him go. He got out of the car and waved to her through the window. She watched him walk away. There was something jaunty in his step, a young man striding into his future on long, loping legs.

Sorrow

Miriam Batson is sitting at her desk in Minneapolis, looking out the window. Her study is on the second floor, and her view is of the parking lot of the grammar school across the street. The parking lot is covered with snow, and cars are parked on the snow. It's a January day, mild and sunny.

While she looks out the window at the view she sees every day, she is thinking of Edith. Ee-de-ith, they always pronounced it, as if it had three syllables. When Miriam spoke to her folks in South Carolina over the Christmas holidays, they told her Edith was doing poorly—fluid around the heart. Miriam had called a few days before Christmas. In the hullabaloo of shopping, wrapping, and mailing, she hadn't sent any money to Edith in time to reach her by Christmas. She wanted her parents to take cash in a card over to her; then she'd send them a check.

"Oh we were over there just this morning," her father said over long distance.

"I took her a gown with your name on it and slippers from me, and we gave her twenty dollars," her mother said. In their old age, twenty dollars counted to her parents.

"How was she?" Miriam asked, always frightened of what she'd hear. She felt, not for the first time, very far away. That's when they told her Edith had fluid around her heart.

In her younger days, Miriam had entertained fantasies of rescuing Edith from a life of old age and poverty—the life Edith was leading now. She imagined that one day Edith would come and live with her, wherever that might be. She hadn't realized then that she would grow up and leave the South, that her visits home would be infrequent, and that she would have to worry about money. She sometimes thought of tithing a part of her income to Edith. A little extra money each month would surely help out. But she never did. She was afraid of starting something she couldn't keep up, and of course there were always things she wanted to buy for herself.

Edith came to work for her family when Miriam was thirteen, in 1960. When she asked her mother how they found Edith, her mother couldn't recall. There was a network of sorts, white women passing around the names of black women who would work for them, be their maids. That was a long time ago, before Miriam knew the term "black." They used the word "colored" and considered it a kindness.

They had always had maids, a string of them, essential to their existence, it seemed. Neva was the first one Miriam "remembers." There is an old home movie of them visiting Miriam's grandmother in Texas. Neva had accompanied them on the trip to help their mother take care of Linda and Miriam. There is Miriam, one year old, learning to walk. It is toward Neva that Miriam stumbles. Neva, a handsome young black woman in a starched white uniform in the hot Texas sun, holding out her arms to Miriam.

Next came Bessie, who left them suddenly to go up North. Or is that just Miriam's imagination? It seems there came a day when Bessie didn't come to work, and when Miriam's mother called—or did she drive to Bessie's house?—someone told them she had left, gone up North, without telling them. Miriam's mother hurt and angry. But Miriam was so young, and it is a nebulous memory, like a dream that dissipates on awakening. What Miriam does remember is a big, powerful woman, Bessie, in the red room, ironing. It is peaceful, a sunny weekday morning, and there's a string of rock candy growing in a glass. Bessie ironing and ironing, her arms muscled and hard like a man's.

Then there was Alma, a teenage girl with long fingernails painted bright pink or red. Miriam and Linda were used to older maids, motherly types, and Alma was so young—dangerous, they sensed, for might she not have the same desires that they had, to go outside whenever they liked, to be free of work, to play? Miriam and Linda wanted to touch her painted fingernails, so long they curled over at the tips, and Alma let them. But those nails were unsettling, signaling that maybe Alma didn't want to be a maid, didn't want to spend her days washing, ironing, cooking and cleaning.

After Alma came Carolyn, who worked for them many years. She didn't live too far away, but of course her house was outside their neighborhood, in a field behind a mill. Carolyn had children of her own, whom Miriam and Linda would see when their mother took her home. Linda and Miriam would eye those children, and Carolyn's children would eye them back, curiously, but from a great distance. Miriam and Linda would ask Carolyn about them, but not too much. They didn't want to know too much.

They had those kids' mama all day and their own mama too, a wealth of mamas, too many, they knew. So they didn't ask too much.

Edith came into their lives after Carolyn. She didn't have a family—perfect, from their point of view. They could be her family; she could give and give to them. She was short, her skin a deep mahogany hue, and she seemed to be composed of balls. Her head was one perfect sphere, her black hair short and slicked flat against her skull; she wore large, round glasses behind which her eyes bulged; her nose was bulbous, her breasts full globes under her uniform. Top-heavy, she had small hips and skinny little legs. Her hands were gnarled with arthritis, but was that early on, or only later, as she aged?

She'd come in the basement door wearing some simple cotton housedress. The first thing she'd do was change into her uniform, white with a blue or black apron, or, on special occasions, such as dinner parties, black with a white apron. She wore bedroom slippers at work, the backs crunched down so she could slip her feet in easily, those feet that hurt her with their hard knobs and bunions. Maids stood on their feet most of the day. Only an infrequent job like polishing the silver accommodated sitting down. Edith must have been middle-aged when she came to them. She was neither young nor old, and like Miriam's own parents, she stayed that way for years.

Her parents were the kind of people who were good to their maids. They had nice manners where maids were concerned. But certain conventions had to be observed, were observed, without questioning. Edith never ate with them. She ate after they did, in the kitchen, and there were separate dishes for colored people, for Edith and Van, who did the yard. When they drove her home, Edith sat in the back seat, never up front with Miriam's mother, and usually Miriam rode in the back too. When she got old enough to drive, Miriam always asked Edith to sit in the front seat with her (and she did, but did that make it Edith's choice?). It was the mid-sixties then, and things were starting to change. Miriam would take her home to Sycamore Street, to her little house, Miriam's mother's big Buick taking up the whole narrow rutted street, and then she'd drive home, back to that other world.

Now it is spring, April, and because it has been a mild winter, the snow is all gone. There are feathery buds on the elms, and children play in the schoolyard, sending up a din of noise, a long, sustained note of exuberant joy.

Miriam's mother called that morning to tell her that Edith had died. She had been sick with heart trouble for about seven weeks; in the hospital the last two. Miriam's family didn't even know it.

All those afternoons when Miriam would come home from junior high and high school, and Edith would be there. After Miriam went away to college and then graduate school in California, whenever she'd come home she'd listen in the early morning for some noise from the basement, the opening of the screen door or the start of the washing machine. She'd rise out of bed, throw on her robe, and go down to see Edith. They'd embrace, laughing and talking. What would they say to one another? They'd use whatever words were at hand. It didn't matter what was said. It was always that moment, the reunion.

For the last several years, Edith only worked for her parents on special occasions. In their old age, her parents couldn't afford to pay her regularly. They kept in touch with Edith through Willie Mae, her best friend who lived down the street. Since Edith didn't have a phone, they'd call Willie Mae whenever they wanted to reach Edith. It was Willie Mae who had called to let Miriam's mother know that Edith had died.

After her parents got old and could no longer hire Edith, Miriam always went over to see her whenever she was home. She'd call Willie Mae to let Edith know she was coming, and then she'd drive over to her house. They'd stand in Edith's red-dirt yard to visit, or lean against Miriam's mother's car. Once Miriam sat on Edith's open porch; she never went inside. Miriam took her picture that day: Edith on the porch, sitting next to a huge Christmas candle, an outdoor decoration Miriam's folks no longer wanted. That day Edith's insurance man came, a young white man, maybe ten years younger than Miriam. While Edith went inside, he and Miriam sat on the bench on the porch, and made polite Southern conversation. Then Edith came out with her seventeen dollars, crumpled-up bills in her old red billfold, and paid him. He praised "Miss Edith" for being such a fine person, and Miriam chimed in. That was the way they talked.

One time when Miriam was home, she took Edith out to lunch. She wanted to treat her, the way she would a favorite aunt or grandmother. She picked Edith up a little after one, and Miriam was nervous. She had never taken a black person out to lunch before in Greenville, where she remembered riding in the bus to town as a child with Carolyn, who had to sit in the back, keeping an eye on Miriam and Linda up in the whites-only section. In Miriam's mind it was still 1954 in South Carolina. She had grown up and gone away, time had passed, progress had been made, but Miriam couldn't imagine that anything had changed in her hometown. She knew the rules so well.

But there they were, Edith and Miriam, going out to

lunch. It still surprised her that in Greenville, blacks had civil rights. Black people went about town the same as any white person. They ate in the same restaurants, they went to the mall, they had good jobs, their pictures were in the newspaper, they were anchors on the evening news. Even though Miriam took such things for granted up North, in Greenville it still surprised her. It always frightened her in that first instant to see black people where they never used to be. She was afraid for them.

Lost in her own hometown, which had grown and changed so much since Miriam lived there, she drove downtown, from habit and because she could find it. So many businesses had moved to the mall, and downtown was now almost abandoned. Main Street, where her father's radio and TV store had been, where the whole life of their town had once thrived (white on one end, black on the other) might have been the main street of a town she never knew. She parked in front of what used to be the best department store, Ivy's. The space had been subdivided into a number of little fledging stores, one of them a delicatessen. It was deserted inside and Miriam felt relief. She worried that Edith might feel ill at ease, since she herself did. But Edith seemed less self-conscious than Miriam. She had a demure way, passive and acquiescing, and yet, underneath, there was desire. Edith wanted things. Miriam knew it, had always known it. She had learned to read the signs, interpret, extrapolate. Edith wanted to be treated.

She ordered a roast beef sandwich. Miriam had only seen her eat at their house, and when they had meat, it was cooked well done, the way her parents, country people like Edith, liked it. The roast beef piled high on a French bun the white girl behind the counter handed Edith in a plastic basket was a shocking raw pink. But Edith took the basket. She was not about to refuse what was offered.

They sat at a little wrought iron table in ice cream parlor chairs. Edith had never been big, but in old age she had shrunk. Gravity and hard work had forced her head down into her shoulders, which were small, but her breasts were still large. Her legs were even skinnier now and had a gray cast, as if rubbed in ash. She was utterly familiar to Miriam and yet strange too, foreign almost, as Miriam watched her arthritic fingers pick up that big sandwich. Edith's eyes, which bulged as though from a goiter condition, never stayed on Miriam's for more than an instant, as if she were shy or afraid to look a white person directly in the face (*but it's me*, Miriam longed to say). They fell into one of their usual conversations, with Miriam soliciting information about Edith's welfare: did she have enough coal for the winter, was she getting her food stamps, how was Willie Mae? Edith was a willing, even voluble talker, though hard to understand, speaking a kind of Southern black rural dialect that Miriam's ear had grown unaccustomed to. The lunch seemed to be a success, and yet as they sat there, Miriam felt troubled. Something in her cried out, *Why can't we just be ourselves?* But of course that's exactly what they were being, exactly who they couldn't help but be.

As they were eating, two other people came in, a young white woman and a young black woman in their twenties, on a coffee break. They must have worked together, perhaps at the Social Security office next door. Miriam felt shocked to see them, black and white together so casually in her hometown, and then she understood that some things had changed.

Those women were operating under a new order, and Edith and Miriam, try as they might, belonged to the old order. They were the dinosaurs, the damaged ones, two about-to-become-extinct creatures from another time, a different era. The world had changed for the better, but not in time for them.

Today Miriam drives slowly down Sycamore Street in Greenville. It's a Monday morning in July, and she's on her way to pick up Willie Mae and Buster. She tries to get a good look at Edith's house as she creeps by in her parents' old Buick, and she tries to remember if Edith ever lived in any other house in all those years she worked for Miriam's family. Did she live in this little house when she first came to work for them? Miriam forces herself to look at it. She's been taught from an early age not to embarrass herself and others by seeing what is obviously there. But now she looks and sees. It's a frame house, the wood a faint, peeling blue, the simplest of structures, raised about three feet off the ground on a crumbling cement foundation. A path is worn across the red-dirt yard, and rickety wooden steps lead up to the porch. Miriam would stop the car here and wait for Edith. She was usually ready, watching, but if she didn't come right out, Miriam would go up and knock on the door. She'd never honk. She remembers watching Edith come down those precarious stairs many times. Nothing to hold on to.

She pulls up in front of the house that she thinks is Willie Mae's. She'd called Willie Mae when she got home this time to see if she would show her where Edith was buried.

Willie Mae had described her house to Miriam—the one with the screen porch. This time Miriam doesn't look, doesn't stare. She pretends that where poor black people live is perfectly normal and perfectly fine. She jumps out of the car and goes to the steps. The porch door is open. An old man is reading the paper on the porch, and he hardly glances at her. Further inside, she sees a woman she knows is Willie Mae. In her navy blue skirt and plain white blouse, she looks strong and stoic, a person of character. She calls to Miriam that she'll be there in a moment. Miriam nervously asks the man on the porch if he is Buster.

"Naw, Buster's in there."

Miriam sees another man, old, white-haired, sitting at the table just inside with a mug of coffee. He seems in no hurry, or maybe he's having a hard time getting going. He nods and speaks to her.

Miriam knew from Edith that a man, Buster, lived with her, but the nature of this relationship was never made explicit. Was he like a husband or a roomer? Miriam wasn't sure. She couldn't tell. How little she knew of Edith's life! All those years she came to Miriam's house, where she saw so much, but then she'd disappear, back into her own life, as if going through a door, shutting it behind her.

Miriam hangs at the bottom of the stairs, waiting for Willie Mae. She has brought Willie Mae a frozen cooked turkey breast. Miriam hands it to her, stuttering out some instructions on how to defrost it. Willie Mae carries it back into the house, and Miriam hurries to the car to open the doors for her and Buster.

Buster sits in the back, Willie Mae in the front. Buster is wearing a bright yellow acrylic sweater and his eyes are red and rheumy, those of a sick man. Beside Miriam, Willie Mae is dignified, solemn, her white hair pulled back in a bun, a scattering of black moles on the milk chocolate of her sculpted face. When she glances over at Miriam, her eyes move quickly and searchingly, as if to assess. She sits straight in the seat, her hands on her knees. Miriam asks her if she got some rest over the weekend; she had sounded so tired on the phone. She tells Miriam she had to work two jobs on Friday because one of the women she works for was fixing to go out of town and needed help getting her clothes ready. She had to stand on her feet all day, and she has trouble with them, swelling and aching like they do.

Miriam makes conversation, but what she really wants to know is *How did Edith die?* Finally she asks, and Willie Mae tells her, gravely and in sorrow, how Edith got sick and how her doctor wasn't doing a thing for her, so Buster took her to his doctor, and he put her right in the hospital.

From the back seat Buster says, "I told him she was my sister."

She had a cardiac arrest in the hospital, but they were able to get her heart started again. About two weeks later, she had another attack, and they couldn't save her. "I hated to see her with all those tubes stuck in her," Willie Mae says sorrowfully.

Buster gives Miriam directions out of town. She asks questions, hesitantly, about Edith. But if she doesn't ask, how will she ever know? She gets the story of how Willie Mae went to live in Anderson County when she was a girl and stayed with Edith's mother. Nothing is explained, elaborated on. Willie Mae answers, but she doesn't tell much. Miriam hungrily asks about Edith's mother: *Was she nice, a good woman?* Oh she was nice all right. *Did you know her father?* I knew him.

And you, Buster?

"I lived over in Anderson County too, we all went to the same church," Buster offers as they glide through the quiet countryside.

Miriam wants to know more about Edith, more about her life and death, but she finds it hard to ask questions. She doesn't know how much is too much; she doesn't want to press or offend Willie Mae, who is, after all, doing her a favor. Miriam is afraid Willie Mae is accommodating her, as she has had to accommodate white people all her life. She answered their questions when she had to, but she kept much back. She won't let Miriam in. Miriam asks her how many children she has: five, and twelve grandchildren, and she doesn't know how many great-grandchildren. She allows a dry laugh. Miriam asks her about her daughter, Diane, the one who has the good job in a corporation.

The country they're passing through was probably cotton fields at one time. Miriam can't help but think of the history of this land. When she traced her family tree, she saw that there had been slave owners in her family. She had wanted to believe that her great-grandfathers, small-time farmers who fought in the Civil War, wouldn't have been able to afford slaves.

Now there is nothing planted here, just open space broken by an occasional suburban brick house or doublewide trailer set far back from the road. Here and there is an old wooden barn about to fall down. Miriam tries to see the land as Edith knew it as a girl, and she can't think it's much changed. They turn left off County Road 8 at Brown's Country Store, and the road winds into woods; they rise and fall. This is the landscape Miriam loves best in all the world—even though it breaks her heart—this little piece of the upper Piedmont of South Carolina.

They have arrived at the church, only Miriam is going too fast to make the sudden turn, so she drives on a ways until she can turn around. Buster watches for her out the back window, but there are no other cars on this road. When they get back to the church, Miriam is disappointed to see there is a chain across the drive, barring their way. She doesn't know what this barrier will mean to their journey. But Willie Mae says they can walk. Buster will wait in the car. Later today he'll go in for dialysis. Miriam looks back at him anxiously. She lets down the electric window.

From the back seat, she gets the artificial arrangement of flowers her parents have put together. On its Styrofoam base, it has ridden upright and secure in a yellow plastic dishpan.

Up ahead is a red brick church with a modest white steeple. It's a newer-looking church, maybe from the seventies. As they slowly walk up the asphalt drive, Willie Mae tells Miriam that they used to come to church here in a different building, the one before this one. Behind the church is the graveyard. It has not been kept up. At the sight of it, Willie Mae sighs. She looks around. They stand at the edge of the burial ground, with its neglected air of past grief and parting, of rest and oblivion. There are old gravestones and wreaths gone to ruin, their silk bows paled by the elements, some of them toppled over. It's a small graveyard, edged on one side by forest, but through a few thin pines, Miriam sees what seems to be a pasture and someone's red brick house.

"I hope I can remember ..." Willie Mae says, stepping forward into the tall grass, looking around. "Seems it was over this-a-way ..."

Miriam's heart is in a clutch. What if they can't find it? She hadn't counted on this.

She looks around for a fresh grave, for evidence of a burial last spring, and suddenly her eyes find it, a raw red mound, small and obscure, camouflaged by dead flowers gone the color of fall. There is a little placard close to the ground, a piece of typed paper protected by plastic, in a small rectangular metal frame: "Edith Earl." She feels shocked. Edith doesn't even have a gravestone. Miriam absorbs this discovery. No gravestone. Her place marked by something as insubstantial as paper, plastic, aluminum.

Willie Mae joins her. They stand for a moment looking at Edith's grave. The arrangements from the funeral are in a collapse of decay. No one has been here since the burial. Silently, they begin to pull off the old dead wreaths with their long rusted metal legs. At the far end of the cemetery is a big pile of old wreaths. She and Willie Mae start carrying the arrangements over to the pile, stepping through tangled vines and high grass, trying not to tread on any of the graves. They make several trips, and then Willie Mae begins, tentatively, to pull out a long vine from the top of the grave. They haven't brought gloves, but they pull all the other weeds, which come up easily, willingly, from the soft earth.

They mostly work in silence. Any conversation has to do with their task at hand. They know so well what to do that it doesn't have to be discussed. They will clear Edith's grave, they will put things in order, they will secure the new arrangement. But the red dirt is too soft, the coat hangers go in with no resistance and won't anchor the flower arrangement. Willie Mae and Miriam consider this situation. They begin to look around.

Miriam retrieves one of the old arrangements from the rubbish pile. Willie Mae takes it in her strong hands and bends the metal legs until they come apart. Together they are able to push the metal sticks through the Styrofoam down deep into the grave.

They stand then for a few moments in silence. To control her emotions, Miriam concentrates on the peacefulness of the countryside, the quiet of the graveyard. Beside her Willie Mae has her head bowed. After a little while, they start the walk back to the car.

Buster has the back door open. The car smells of cigarette smoke. He and Willie Mae exchange a few comments while Miriam backs out of the church drive and starts down the road. Then Buster says, "I just know Edith was smiling when she saw you coming. 'Here comes my Miriam,' she'd be saying. She sure did love you."

"Yes she did," Willie Mae echoes.

These words, so full of kindness, crack open Miriam's heart.

Willie Mae and Buster allow Miriam her grief. She struggles to compose herself, to drive the car. She fumbles for a Kleenex in her purse and wipes her eyes.

But Miriam can't stop crying. She hardly knows what she's crying for, it all seems so big, so deep. It's Edith, her death, her life, it's the whole thing, the whole South, the whole horrible crime of it, the whole ...

For a few moments she weeps as if she'll never stop.

Then she is over it. The crying part, though not the sorrow.

Enormously Valuable

The phone call came unexpectedly on a Monday morning.

"Miriam, I hate to have to give you some bad news. We've hired someone else for the job."

"Oh no!" Miriam exclaimed. "That is disappointing!" But in a second she composed herself. "Can you tell me who?"

"His name is Gary Provo," Rupert Jones intoned in his British accent. "Thank you for not yelling at me, Miriam."

"You know I wouldn't do that," Miriam said politely, perfunctorily. But even in her dazed state she was puzzled. Why would he think she'd yell at him? Miriam was hardly a yeller. Later, when she had yelled at him in a sense, she would remember this little exchange.

"He's got a collection of stories coming out this fall," Rupert continued. As head of the creative writing program at the big Midwestern university where Miriam taught as an adjunct, he brought a little taste of Oxford or Cambridge to the sprawling urban campus.

"We just felt he had an irresistible combination of things. Irresistible. He comes very highly recommended. It wasn't so much no to you as yes to him. It was a very prayerful decision, I can tell you that. It went back and forth, back and forth. You did so well in the interview, we were all so proud of you, and that just made it all the harder."

"I see," Miriam said blankly.

"You know we value you enormously. I'll do everything I can to give you a good teaching schedule next year."

She was eager to get off the phone. She had conducted herself with sufficient dignity, but she could only hold on so long. When she hung up, she burst into tears. But at least she hadn't cried on the phone.

It was difficult to go back to the university the next day. The long-awaited opportunity for a real job, albeit a temporary two-year one, had evaporated for her. Miriam knew such a job was no big deal, though that did not seem to diminish her desire for it. It was essentially the same work she was doing now, and had been doing for a number of years, as an adjunct, only this had been a position, a real job with benefits, at more than twice what she was being paid now.

There was a departmental announcement in her box about the writer who had been hired. Miriam read through it quickly, and then she read it through more slowly. For one thing, she was surprised that they had hired a man. For the last ten years, the university had been under a class action decree to redress past sex discrimination. Miriam had heard Rupert say that if they had two roughly equally-qualified candidates, they were required to hire a woman. She had known there might very well be better candidates than she—it was, after all, a national search. But Miriam was not exactly a slouch. And she was already here, doing the job, "enormously valuable," as Rupert was always telling her.

Gary Provo, she read, had gotten his MFA from Iowa, and was currently a Stegner Fellow at Stanford. His first book of stories was coming out in the fall. He had published a couple of stories in literary magazines. Up to that point, Miriam thought, their resumes were rather similar. She too had been a Stegner Fellow at Stanford, she had published a collection of short stories with good national reviews, had had a number of short stories and nonfiction pieces in magazines. But what stopped her in her tracks—she felt herself come to a halt—was that he only had one year of teaching experience. That was it. A deep frown formed in her brain and expressed itself on her forehead, which wrinkled into a knot.

She brought the department announcement home to her husband, Ted, and together they tried to make sense of things.

"Maybe it's because he has a book coming out in the fall," Ted said. "That makes him hot. Your book has been out for several years—three, isn't it?—so it's not so hot."

"Whose side are you on?" Miriam said. "What really gets me is that I'm already teaching here. Enormously valuable, according to Rupert. This guy's an unknown—unproved—stranger!"

"Of course the other thing," Ted said carefully, "is that they may think he's a better writer than you."

"God!" Miriam said. She looked at Ted bleakly. Her whole sense of herself as a writer—what she had worked for, built up, accomplished—felt about to blow out the door.

Not that she didn't believe other writers could be better than she. She did! She was the first to believe it. She was always ready and willing to believe it. "They" were better and she was nothing. Or if not exactly nothing, then not good enough. Not—fill-in-the-blank—enough.

"But what about teaching! He's taught one year and I've taught twelve, thirteen, fourteen, I don't even know anymore. A lot. And I'm a really good teacher! How could they totally disregard teaching?"

"Their prerogative, I guess," Ted said sadly.

"I've been screwed!" Miriam exclaimed.

So that was that. The decision was made, the committee had spoken, Miriam had not been chosen, life goes on. Because it was only a two-year temporary job, a committee, rather than the full department, had made the decision. Something must have come out in the interview that clearly defined this Gary guy as the superior choice. Miriam thought back to her own interview. They had pitched her a soft ball on the first question: asking her about teaching, of all things! She had told them how she had dealt with her graduate class that morning, and her answer impressed even her. She was in top form, and when it was over, she had a hard time imagining that she wouldn't get the job.

But she hadn't gotten it. What a shock! Things like this were not supposed to happen to her! Why not? She had been around academia long enough to know that people—often the best people—got screwed all the time.

But still, things like this were not supposed to happen to *her*! WHY NOT? Because, because, because ... because she was nice! She didn't ask for too much (only a temporary job), she was an excellent, overly conscientious worker, cheerful, gracious, modest, supportive, a team player, reasonable, didn't make waves ... She knew how to be nice. Her whole upbringing had been about being nice. Her mother had never articulated the reason a girl had to be nice and maybe had forgotten or never known it herself, having accepted it *prima facie* from her own mother. But now Miriam grasped the underlying rationale: to avoid getting hurt. Her mother hadn't taught her to be tough; she had taught her to be nice. As if that could protect her. And maybe it could, in a parlor. But not in an English Department. Nice was nice, but no defense against getting screwed. In fact, it just made it easier, Miriam now saw. Rupert had thought, since Miriam was always so nice, that she'd get screwed and say thank you very much! If he thought of her at all.

Still, no use to get so worked up. What good would it do? Better to just wait and see what she would be offered for the coming year. After all, Rupert had said he'd do his best to give her a good schedule. She'd get over this … Maybe she was overreacting, even. Miriam loved to be measured, reasonable, mature and she was not entirely comfortable with her present feelings of outrage. Better to just get over it and go on.

When she got the letter regarding next year from the creative writing office, she saw that she had been offered the usual three courses, but one of them was a night course in Rochester. Rochester! She'd have to drive an hour and a half each way—at night in the winter! And of course the salary was the usual piddley-shit adjunct insult, with no benefits. The new man would be making more than twice what she would make, with benefits, to teach three courses and do a little advising. Burn.

• • •

That night Miriam told Ted about the three courses and Rochester.

The next morning, Ted said, "You know, you might have a sex discrimination claim." He had slept on it, he said, because he hadn't wanted to say anything right away. He realized once he said it, there would be no turning back. He knew Miriam, he said, knew she'd have to follow through. In some ways Miriam was a plaintiff just waiting to happen. All those years in the women's movement. Not that she was an angry radical, a time bomb just waiting to go off. Mostly she got along just fine in the world, which she did not see as "us" and "them." On the other hand, she did tend to view things in feminist terms, to be testy about anything that smacked of sexism. In that way, Miriam thought she was no different from most of the women she knew.

Sex discrimination. It wasn't as if Miriam hadn't thought of that. But she had put it out of her mind. She didn't believe that the committee had sat around thinking they ought to hire a man instead of a woman. Not in this day and age. Not after what the university had been through with the sex discrimination decree, having its consciousness raised in the most painful and public way. But the committee had been composed of four men and two women. It didn't seem exactly a coincidence that such a male-dominated committee would choose a male. And they really did have to see Gary Provo as being far superior to Miriam in order to hire him over her. Wasn't it quite possible that they brought to their judgments of his writing vs. Miriam's some male bias? After all, these were men who had cut their teeth on Joyce, Conrad, Melville, Hemingway.

But Miriam wanted to be fair. She didn't want to leap to conclusions, especially polemical ones. Miriam wasn't particularly political. She was too moderate by nature, too—reasonable. Too nice.

She could switch channels in her head, one perspective being "theirs," Rupert and the committee's (as if they were a rock group), that this was a simple matter: They had hired the best candidate, the best person (man?) for the job for reasons that made perfectly good sense, and she should just accept that and get on with things; and another perspective, being hers, that she had been screwed, that it had to do in some fundamental way with her being a woman, and that women were always in danger of getting screwed. If you let them get away with it. If you didn't say *Excuse me. I think we have a problem here.*

Because Ted was a lawyer, Miriam knew a fair number of lawyers, some of them women. By that afternoon, after a couple of phone calls, she had made an appointment with one of the best employment-discrimination attorneys in town. Betsy Airondale's name kept coming up again and again. She was, as a friend at the office of Labor Relations told Miriam, a person with a brilliant legal mind and a lot of common sense. That, Miriam thought, was the combination she needed.

She and Ted went to see Betsy Airondale the following Monday. Miriam had sent her the job advertisement, the two vitas, and a copy of her book. When Betsy came out to meet them, Miriam liked her immediately. She had a kind, intelligent face, and a voice that was warm and low. Miriam thought how much she liked women, at least women like Betsy Airondale. She liked women who were unabashedly for other women.

Betsy laid out the legal possibilities. Sex discrimination would be hard to prove, because the burden of proof would be on Miriam. Equal work for equal pay looked better; and there was some possibility of looking into some new contractual law regarding affirmative action. She said one thing she could do was steer Miriam through the internal processes at the university. They would recognize her name, Betsy said lightly but meaningfully.

"I just have to ask you one thing," Miriam said at the end, as they were finishing up. "I know it may sound ridiculous, but am I being ridiculous? Am I off the wall?"

Betsy looked at her sympathetically. "You know," she said, "it's sad that you have to ask that. Women get screwed all the time, and then they think that somehow it's their fault. So no, you're not crazy."

Ah, Miriam thought. I didn't really think so.

A week had passed since she had gotten the letter about her appointment for next year. The time had come for Miriam and Rupert to have a little talk. He had noticed, he said, that Miriam hadn't responded to the offer. He could tell, he said, that she was unhappy.

"You've withdrawn a bit from things," Rupert said.

They were sitting in Rupert's office, which was just around a partition from Miriam's office. They weren't exactly friends, but they were "colleagues," as Rupert was always so quick to say. He had been so lavish in his praise and support of her. Why hadn't he pulled for her in the committee meeting about the hire? As director of the program, his opinion would have carried great weight.

"You're right," Miriam said. "I am unhappy. I'm unhappy with my schedule for next year. That course in Rochester—to have to drive that distance at night in winter! I'm unhappy that I'm being paid basically subsistence wages." She was warming up. "I'm unhappy because I feel I'm better qualified than the man you hired for the two-year position. I'm unhappy because you're going to pay him more than twice what you're offering me for essentially the same work! I'm unhappy, Rupert, because I have a ton of teaching experience and he has one year, and this is a teaching job. I'm unhappy that you've told me umpteen times how 'enormously valuable' I am, and you didn't put your money where your mouth was. So, yes, Rupert, I am unhappy!"

Rupert had gradually been shrinking back in his desk chair, as if the back might give way, like a secret door, and he'd be out of there.

"Miriam," he exclaimed. "I'm staggered! Staggered. After I've been so good to you!"

"Rupert," Miriam said. "Let me put it this way. I feel I've been discriminated against. Sex discrimination." She might as well have pulled out a gun and pointed it at him, so alarmed did he look. Despite the heat of the moment, Miriam observed his reaction coolly. She relished a feeling she didn't often have: righteous anger. Power. Standing up for herself. "For starters, you and the committee completely ignored the affirmative-action stipulation."

"Miriam, I can't believe my ears. The way you're turning on me. After I've been so good to you! I've always given you three courses every year, which is more than most of our adjuncts get."

"That's true," Miriam said. "And in the past I've been happy to have them. I knew it was the best I could get as an adjunct. This is my job, Rupert, what I do to make money. And it wasn't exactly one way, you know. As you may recall, I've often filled in for full professors at a fraction of their pay. Perhaps I was naive but what choice did I have? You know how tight the market is, how many writers there are around here looking for teaching jobs. And now you're bringing in an unproven, unknown stranger to do the job I've been doing and paying him a lot more money."

"Miriam, I really can't believe my ears." He shook his head in amazement. "After I've been so good to you."

"Rupert," Miriam said in a steely voice, "I'm going to have to ask you not to say that again."

Miriam stood up. "I'd say we're at an impasse here," she said. "We'll have to talk later." She had the feeling that she had lobbed a grenade into the room. As soon as she stepped into the hall, she realized she had cystitis. The urge to urinate was urgent and unnatural. She hadn't had a cystitis attack in twenty years, she contemplated as she peed furiously in the women's room. That little encounter had upset her whole metabolism.

By ten o'clock that night she was at an all-night pharmacy getting a prescription for a sulfur drug. She told one of her women friends about her sudden mysterious attack, and the friend looked up "cystitis" in a New Agey book that listed physical ailments and the emotional condition connected to them. "Urinary infections," the friend read to Miriam over the phone. "Pissed off. Especially at a member of the opposite sex. Blaming others."

Ah. So.

Still ... blaming others. Miriam brooded over this. She was definitely pissed off at a member of the opposite sex, Rupert by name, but she didn't believe in "blaming others." She did not see herself as a victim. Perhaps she should really be blaming herself for what happened. Or at least not blaming others. Maybe she had it all wrong!

She called Ted at work. Blaming others, she repeated. "Does that mean I'm wrong to blame others?"

"If someone dropped a concrete block on your head ..."

"Oh. Okay. Right. Got it."

• • •

She thought of the beefy backs of the male professors in the department. She remembered sitting behind them at a departmental lecture recently, and how they formed a veritable mountain of maleness in front of her. She couldn't see around them, couldn't see the speaker. She was sure they felt entitled to be there, to take up all the room.

Oh this was awful thinking! It was unfair, beneath her! Not all the men in the department had beefy backs! Some, she assumed, were okay, fine even. Weren't they? She wasn't sure. She realized that she didn't trust a one of them. And it was this maleness, this sense of power and entitlement that existed in the department, that made her feel this way. They were a dying breed, the middle-aged, aging men of the department, and they were holding on for all they were worth, which wasn't much in some cases. But it was also true that things were changing. New blood was flowing in in the form of women, younger men who were more enlightened, a few people of color (when they could lure them to Minnesota, not exactly a hotbed of multiculturalism).

Maybe this was just a matter of ego. Her pride was hurt. Raised Southern and female, Miriam was not particularly comfortable with ego. It made her feel guilty to have one, though have one she did. She thought a lot, at times, of herself. That had come, in part, from publishing her book, which some people loved. They said they loved it, at least. Not everyone, of course. But some. Although maybe that was just another variation on "enormously valuable." And then, too, there were just all the years—they hadn't counted for nothing. She might have started out as a quivering mass of female insecurity but over the years something inside had solidified, gotten a grip. She could feel this mysterious part of herself as if it were a rod inside her, holding her up. There might be layers still of uncertainty, inadequacy, self-doubt—there were!—but she also sensed that rod inside as something solid, forged by fire into metal.

After her meeting with Rupert, Miriam got a call from the assistant director of the creative writing program. They would be glad, he told her, to exchange the Rochester course for a graduate-level memoir course in town if she liked.

She had moved the mountain an inch.

It's not easy to move a mountain an inch.

But it was not enough.

Miriam was in her office. It was awkward, because Rupert and she practically shared the space. There was a partition between them, but they shared a common entrance, the only two people in that large room. Miriam had always gotten along well with Rupert. They had a genial, if remote, relationship. He was a poet, a potentially appealing and sympatico sensibility that had, unfortunately, to dwell in Rupert's somewhat messed-up masculine personality. She could hear him bumbling around in his office, and finally he stuck his head around the corner and Miriam asked him to come in.

"I've had a horrible week since we last talked," he said. There was a chair available, which students sat in when they came for conferences, but he didn't take it. He stood, towering over Miriam as she sat at her desk. He was large, tall, physically imposing. "This has been very painful for me," he said. "I haven't been able to sleep well. The things you said really hurt me." Miriam had figured it would be painful for Rupert, who saw himself as a good guy who did the right things, liberal, sensitive, a poet after all, not that that guaranteed anything. But Miriam knew a thing or two about pain herself. She was fascinated, even as she sat pinned to her chair, in the way this had become *his* pain.

"Rupert, would you like to sit down?"

"No, no," he said, "I just wanted you to know how badly I've been feeling about all this."

Later, Miriam would remember this moment, not from what was said, but because of the body language, the way he didn't give up the advantage of standing over her, talking down to her, as it were.

"Rupert," she said, "can you see this from my point of view at all?"

"Oh yes!" he said. "I've been carrying on very active dialogues with you in my mind."

"And I with you," Miriam said. But neither of them seemed able to say anything now.

There was a terrible weight in the room. Both Miriam and Rupert were extremely somber. Miriam felt crushed by the situation, of causing such a terrible dispute, of being in conflict with someone she had known so long, whom she had liked well enough. They had never been friends, but they had been friendly always, and they had worked together. She wished he would sit down. But she saw that that was the problem, in a nutshell. He wanted, needed, and would maintain his "standing." He had his position; he wouldn't back down.

But neither would Miriam. She knew as well as she knew her own name that she wasn't going to drop it. She was still flabbergasted on some level at the way she had been treated. She saw that she was making a choice. She could choose to get over this, the way she was "supposed to." But why not, every once in a while, pick your battle—

even if it costs you?

Rupert rattled on—she already knew the script—"enormously valuable ... programmatic decision ... prayerful ..." She sensed that he wanted to talk it away. She knew Rupert, a highly verbal person, and she knew he would want to throw a lot of words into the air, but that he had no intention of doing anything. Just a lot of "prayerful" words which would make him feel better. But this wasn't about self-expression. It was about being screwed.

"I'm going to write you a letter telling you my side of it," Rupert said.

"I would appreciate that," Miriam said.

They were both exceedingly polite, grave, wary.

Sitting there after Rupert left, Miriam felt filled with pain. It was excruciating to her. She wondered if she would be able to go on. She wondered if she was doing the right thing. Wouldn't it just be better to accept things, or go away? Wouldn't it be easier? Or even just take the three courses and concentrate on her writing? That was what she had always wanted, anyway—to write. But how could she separate the life from the writing? The writing had to come out of a self that she valued, respected, protected. How could she write out of a life, a self, that she had allowed to be treated in such a sorry way?

But with a click of the remote control in her head, she switched channels. Of course the people who had made the hiring decision had thought they were making a good decision! Rupert had explained their rationale, how the new man would bring new life to the program, an experimental perspective, and how the majority of the committee had felt they'd be extremely lucky to get him. He came highly recommended. As for the teaching part, well, he was a good writer, so probably he'd be a good teacher.

Miriam could see all that. It made perfect sense; it was a valid position. She was always teaching point of view in her fiction classes, and here was a brilliant example of how the same story looked different depending upon who was telling it. She was sure Rupert had felt he was making the best decision for the program. As director of the program his opinion would carry the most weight—the committee would honor his recommendation, defer to him. She had expected him to stand up for her, to make it known how "enormously valuable" she was. But he hadn't done that. From his perspective, this wasn't even about her.

Ah, there was the rub. How could it not be "about her" when she was someone he knew, supposedly valued? She knew she was not supposed to take it so personally, but to her it was nothing but personal. Rupert might pretend that it was all "objective," or impersonal, but that was just an interpretation, not reality. That was guy talk.

She had a gut-level feeling that she wasn't real to him in some way—as a person, as a human being. He chose to fall back on the notion that he was being "professional," as if that were some great value. Objective. As if there were such a thing! He had said they weren't supposed to take loyalty into account in a hiring decision. Why not? She didn't expect him to hire her because they were friends; they weren't friends. But given that she was as qualified as Gary Provo, she did expect their association to count, for the human connection that came from working together all those years to matter. But that was girl-think. She and Rupert were yelling at each other across a great gender divide.

On Betsy's advice, Miriam began exploring the internal options for seeking some redress, meeting with people inside the university. She was doing as much as she could on her own, to keep the attorney's fees down. Betsy did not come cheap, and Ted, being experienced with how a lawyer's time could add up, had told Betsy from the start what their ceiling was. It was good to have a lawyer with you when you talked to your lawyer, Miriam thought.

Miriam met with Jill Fredolf, the university's Equal Opportunity and Affirmative Action Officer. Her job was to keep the university from being sued, so she might be interested in helping Miriam find an internal remedy.

Jill was a tall, red-haired woman in her fifties. She had a serious, straightforward, almost sorrowful demeanor (all that sex discrimination, Miriam thought), but she was not without warmth or humor. She seemed sympathetic to Miriam's story, and asked the secretary to bring her Miriam's file. There was, she discovered, a target goal of two women in the lecturer position at the university, so the committee had had to disregard that, something they were not supposed to do. She read Miriam Rupert's report giving the reason they had chosen a man over a qualified female candidate: "The committee's preference, first of all, was for the high quality of his fiction—truly masterful in craft and mature and generous in insight." In the space explaining why they had not hired the best female candidate, identified not by name but by number, Rupert had written that "her prose did not have the energy of Mr. X's." Miriam and Jill looked at each other, raising their eyebrows in exactly the same way, as if they were a mirror image one of the other.

Miriam had not yet told Rupert whether she was going to accept the three courses for next year or not. She hadn't gotten the letter he'd promised, explaining his side of things, and she was trying to decide what to do. Betsy had told her not to accept or turn down the courses until she had to, especially until she had met with Jane Steiner, the grievance officer, who was known as a strong feminist. But on Tuesday, back in her office, she got a call from the assistant director of the creative writing program, wanting to know whether or not she was going to take the three courses offered.

"I can't tell you until I've met with the grievance officer," Miriam said.

In a few minutes Rupert came steaming into Miriam's office.

"I hear you're going to be talking to the grievance officer! If you're going to do that, I'm certainly not going to put anything in writing." He towered above her. Why doesn't he just sit down, Miriam wondered tiredly. She realized with a kind of slow amazement that he had expected all this to just go away. Hearing the word "grievance," realizing Miriam was talking to other people about the matter, people who might even see it her way, had raised his awareness a notch. No doubt, Miriam thought, I have "hurt" him again.

"If you insist on taking this through a grievance procedure," he said, "things are going to come out that you're not going to want to hear."

Miriam sat at her desk. The blood left her hands, her feet, her face; everything rushed to the core. She felt in that core her true self, the self that knew better than the self sitting in her desk chair, squelched down by the looming bulk of Rupert, what was going on. "So now we have a threat?"

This clearly knocked him back a bit. He stood there, silent for a moment. Miriam, observing, was fascinated by how they parried and thrust. He had stunned her into a moment of silence, then she had stunned him back.

"You've misunderstood me!" he exclaimed. "It wasn't a threat! That wasn't what I meant at all."

But that was what it had felt like! It had felt like—crude intimidation. *Things are going to come out that she wouldn't want to hear ...*

What could he possibly mean? It wasn't as if he had any dirt on Miriam, no scandals, affairs, improprieties of any sort. The only thing she could think of was that things would be said about her writing!

"Rupert," she said in a rather impassioned way, "people love my book and I don't care what a few academics think of it." As soon as she said it, it became true. She didn't care. In fact, she'd be damned if she was going to let them denigrate her little book! She tried a softer note: "You must realize how vulnerable I am in this situation. How isolated I am. I need to talk to the grievance officer. I have a grievance. That's the procedure."

"Well," he said grudgingly, "you have a right to do that, and no one can stop you."

Miriam ached all over. Another extremely difficult, painful scene.

They agreed the next step was for her to talk to the chair of the English Department. It was becoming clear that they could not talk to each other.

Miriam sat in the office of Christopher Martin-Burke, the chair of the English Department. Christopher was another middle-aged Englishman. He and Miriam had always had a pleasant enough relationship, though Miriam didn't know him well. Their main contact had come when Christopher had showed her a copy of a letter from a couple saying they were funding a $1,000 scholarship in creative writing after seeing Miriam speak at the public library. That was in the good old days, when Miriam was so enormously valuable to the program.

Miriam reminded Christopher of her long history with the department, her good service and excellent reputation as a writer and teacher. She'd never been a troublemaker. Then she told him she planned to file a formal complaint with the university's EOAA office.

Christopher listened quietly and seriously and said that he was basically sympathetic to her situation. He said he saw it as an "adjunct" problem. ("Right," Ted said later, "similar to the galley-slave problem.") He had feared for years that some adjunct would begin to think the university owed him or her something.

"Rupert told me that loyalty couldn't be taken into account in a national search but it seems to me the opposite of loyalty has gone on here. I was at a disadvantage because I was already here, available, known, an insider."

"I've seen the insider passed over many times," Christopher said. "Familiarity breeds contempt"—as if that would make Miriam feel better. "We can offer you the three courses plus some advising, which will increase your salary by $3,000."

"I can't accept that," Miriam said. "I'm making a formal request at this meeting for the exact same job for which you've hired Mr. Provo: three courses plus advising for two years, at the same pay."

"Oh. I see," Christopher said.

Miriam left him a copy of her EOAA complaint. She had risen out of bed in a trance one morning at 5:00 a.m., and written it straight through, nine pages organized into the facts, background, and then taking the issues involved and addressing each one. It had poured out of her with the speed and determination, the certainty of a locomotive.

She glanced back after she left Christopher's office. He was devouring her complaint, rather frantically she thought. He couldn't even wait until she was in the hall. She felt some sense of satisfaction, that she had sent him scurrying so.

She walked over to the administration building, and delivered the complaint to the EOAA office. It was important to her to make a formal complaint. Regardless of what came of it, she wanted it on record: I've been screwed! Leaving the complaint with the secretary, she felt like Martin Luther nailing his edicts to the church door at Wittenberg.

The time had come for Miriam to read the story that Gary Provo had submitted. In the downtown library she found the literary magazine where it had been published. As she began reading, she felt light-headed and her palms began to sweat, the way they did when she was too near the edge of a high cliff or tall building. Provo's words seemed bathed in a golden light—the page itself took on a golden sheen. She thought she heard music, a soundtrack magnifying the moment with the poignant strains of violins.

It was a great story! The best story she had ever read! No, that wasn't true. But it was good. Really good. She felt faint. Provo really was a better writer than she … The committee had been right to hire him over her. No matter that she was a good writer, a good teacher—this one story knocked her whole life to smithereens.

She fled to Ted's office, which luckily was nearby.

"It's over," she said, sitting across from him at his desk, as if she were a client, which in a way, she was. "I give up. Uncle. Provo is a better writer than me." She felt brave and hopeless. It seemed important to tell the truth, not to lie to herself, no matter how it hurt. She believed in honesty, after all.

"Well, you're not exactly chopped liver," Ted said.

"Good, better, best. You're always telling me that these kinds of judgments are subjective. Maybe someone else would like your writing better."

Miriam listened. She was regaining her equilibrium. She remembered how strange she had felt reading Provo's story, as if she might levitate, as if her worst fears had come true. (Years later, she would reread the story, and admire it but also wonder at her earlier reaction—overreaction—how she was so willing to believe his writing was so superior to hers, as if God himself had penned it).

"You see what's happening here," Ted said. "You're buying into their position, their way of seeing things. X is so much better than Y. Based on one story? They give him a two-year job based on one story and no teaching experience?"

"He's taught one year," Miriam said.

"Yeah, and you've taught umpteen and have a great reputation as a teacher. And people did love your book, Miriam. Just because that committee went for this one story of Provo's isn't any reason to throw your whole career overboard. Who you are. What you've done. What you stand for."

"I don't know," Miriam said. "It's like I have two minds. One is what I think of as my own—and that mind is screaming at me that I've been screwed, it makes the same arguments you've been making, that I can't let them get away with this, that I have to stand up for myself. Because if I don't who else will? And if I don't stand up for myself, they get to define me. They get to say who I am, what kind of writer I am, and somehow that will get incorporated into who I am—if I don't say 'No.' No. Like I'm holding my hand out to stop them, to hold them off, to keep them from … hurting me … in some crucial way …

"But I also have this other mind and it's like it's theirs.

I see things their way, I see Provo is a better writer and it doesn't matter about teaching, he's hot and exotic and not from here. So he brings new things to the program and that's what they want. And they get to say! They're the committee. I'm supposed to accept their decision gracefully, even if I lose. I know the values they're operating under—I know them so well, it's not as if I haven't been around the university all these years."

"Look, this is typical in lawsuits," Ted said. "You go up and down. You have moments of doubt. You see the other side. Maybe you lose your nerve. It doesn't seem worth it. But then you buck up. You go back to what you believe. What's important to you. And in this situation, even if you lose, it's important that you stand up for yourself. That you not let them run over you."

"Okay," Miriam said.

Still, she had her doubts. Oh the luxury of being right, of no ambiguity! Self-righteously right. That must be the best position to be in in the world! To be screwed, unambiguously. To be a clear-cut victim, to have black and white enemies, villains, sexist bad guys. But Miriam did not have that luxury. What she had was a position, a need, a hurt ego, pain and anger and ... no small thing ... the law. Maybe it wasn't sex discrimination—not blatant, pure-tee out-and-out sex discrimination. She doubted that it was. Rather, it was subtle and hard to prove; maybe the men on the committee did subconsciously gravitate toward the male, relate and identify more with his fictional persona, a man, than Miriam's, a woman. And the whole matter of judgment in writing! She hated that. Who was "best." Who got to say? And what about teaching? Rupert claimed to care about teaching—he had a good reputation as a teacher himself—and then he completely disregarded that in terms of speaking up for Miriam. But Rupert was the quintessential company man. And Rupert had all the power. A tenured professor, director of the program, he had the system behind him—Miriam didn't stand a chance. Well, she was going to take a stand, that was all. She was going to say, *Excuse me, there's another point of view here, another way of looking at this. I beg to differ. Just wanted you to know.*

A few weeks before the end of the school year, Miriam was notified that she was one of four winners of a distinguished teaching award at the university. The graduate students with whom she'd worked had nominated her. She was the only woman, and the only adjunct. Rupert had written a letter of support (this before they locked horns) saying he had only the highest praise for Miriam as a writer, teacher, and colleague. "I have the utmost trust in her abilities, and only wish we had a permanent position for her here." He closed with "I admire and value her enormously." The award ceremony was bittersweet for Miriam. She was being honored for distinguished teaching, and yet she would not be back next year. In her acceptance speech she thanked the students who had nominated her and written letters on her behalf. She ended by saying that she thought teaching as a value was always vulnerable at a university that put too much emphasis on research and publication, and that she hoped the university would keep saying in various ways and through various acts that excellence in teaching actually counts.

(*Oh how, oh how did I get into this situation!* she couldn't help thinking. *I've become my own worst nightmare—a self-righteous, wounded pontificator!*)

• • •

And then the year was over. Miriam had to pack up her books and files and move out of her office. Her complaint was still in process, with no resolution in sight. It was hard, walking down the steps of the English Department building for the last time. The university had meant so much to her, it had been a big part of her life for many years. She felt she belonged there.

In July a letter came, informing her that, without admitting guilt, the English Department was offering her a one year contract for three courses and advising for the same salary that Mr. Provo was receiving. She had "won," sort of.

Back she went to the university, back up the steps to the English Department in the fall, to teach her courses, and to sit around a conference table with Rupert and Gary Provo and the other creative writing faculty. It was uncomfortable, sure, but Miriam needed the money, and she had, after all, really wanted this job. She thought she deserved it. She and Rupert maintained a civil if strained relationship. But basically they weren't speaking to one another—not beyond what was necessary business. They were both invariably polite and professional during these interchanges. But no small talk, no greetings in the hall.

End of year. Packing up again. But then a surprise. She had been looking around for another job, without much hope, and suddenly she was hired for the coming year to teach at a prestigious private college nearby. She'd be paid twice what she had been paid at the university, receive benefits, and even have a title: Distinguished Visiting Professor. It was only for a year (though the job extended into three years) but it made leaving the university a lot easier. The chair of that English Department was another middle-aged man, only Irish this time instead of English. His wife had loved Miriam's book, as it turned out, and had prevailed on him to hire her.

Coda

As it happened, two years later, Miriam and Ted were flying to England when who should appear coming down the aisle of the 747 but Rupert Jones. He was flying to England too, on the same flight. Well, it was a big plane and once he was past their row, it shouldn't be a problem. Miriam kept her eyes in her book. She and Rupert hadn't spoken since Miriam had left the university, even when they were at the same parties or readings. They had parted without ever making up.

Only what was this? Rupert had the seat directly behind them! Isn't life entertaining! Doesn't life have a great sense of humor! He and Miriam ignored each other for the eight-hour flight, as if they were strangers, which they now were. But in Gatwick, while they were waiting for their luggage, Miriam made herself go over to Rupert and speak to him. Why not at least try to be an adult? They were able to chat amiably about their trips. Finally Miriam indicated she'd better get back to help Ted with the luggage.

"Thank you for speaking to me," Rupert said. Miriam was taken aback. It occurred to her that he had been afraid to speak to her first. Why was that? He was afraid she might yell at him. "Thank you for not yelling at me," he had said a long time ago, when he had first called to tell her they had hired someone else. And of course she had ended up yelling at him, in a way. He must think women are dangerous creatures about to blow up all the time, she thought in amazement.

"Have a good trip, Rupert," Miriam said. And she meant it. In that moment she forgave him, and she forgave herself. When she walked away, she felt lighter than she had in a long time.

Swimming, Snow

For Miriam the winter of her father's death would always be juxtaposed with a summer day. It was the Saturday of Labor Day weekend and she had ridden her bike down to Lake Harriet, near their house in Minneapolis, to the north beach, just beyond the bandstand, where her husband Ted had his sailboat tipped up on shore to clean the hull. Miriam had meant to help with the scrubbing; she had good intentions. But as soon as she saw the water, she wanted to go swimming.

She hadn't been swimming all summer. She didn't know why. It was just that she was always so busy. Doing what? She tried to think. Before her the lake sparkled in the sun. She had just finished teaching a summer school course, and she was working part-time at a bookstore. Then there was Ted, a high-maintenance husband, and lots of women friends, and of course there was writing. It was like a demanding, beloved child. She waded into the water.

She struck out through the sailboats bouncing lightly on their buoys. She passed two female mallards who were swimming there too. Up above the sky was a resplendent blue. Snow-white clouds, cumulus now, would be thunderheads by evening. She floated for a while on her back, the sun on her face. Then she commenced swimming again.

She had spoken to her parents in South Carolina just that morning. Her father had sounded fine, though she noticed that he didn't linger on the phone, as if he found it too much effort to call across the miles about the Southern heat, his tomatoes, Miriam's trip that morning to the farmers' market. Oh! she remembered him saying, I wish I could have gone with you! Well, Miriam wished that too.

After she hung up, she had felt disturbed, restless, and she had a strong feeling that she should get to South Carolina. She had gone upstairs and looked hard at her calendar. She marked off five days in October when she could go. At that moment she remembered a dream: Both her parents had died suddenly, in a plane crash. They dropped out of the sky and were gone. Then she was in their old house having to go through their things and dispose of what had been her parents' material life.

Now, swimming, Miriam lost track of time and distance. But suddenly something frightened her, a dark shadow passing over. She jerked up, trying to touch bottom that wasn't there. How far away the shore was! There was the tipped-up hull of the sailboat, a large portion of which was now a bright blue, the rest a dull green, and Ted's tiny figure bent over a bucket. But the shadow? Looking up, she saw that a plane had passed over. With her earplugs in and her head in the water, she hadn't heard it.

When she returned to the beach, she was pleasantly tired. She spread her towel on the sand and lay down. The sun warmed her, smiling on her. So this is what it is like, she thought happily, to relax. Relaxation was not a big part of Miriam's life. She was always in a hurry, always busy, always striving, achieving, or at least trying. It had to do, she thought, with being a woman, living in a city, in the last decade of the century. Then she was asleep.

When she woke it was late afternoon. She felt deeply

refreshed, as if she had traveled to some distant, restful place. Her limbs felt loose and light, her mind empty and clear. She couldn't remember such a feeling of well-being. She told herself she would come swimming again, soon.

When she came in from her lunch break at the bookstore the next day, she immediately encountered a difficult customer. Most people who bought books were polite and good humored, but this woman was the exception. She had ordered a book that *Books in Print* listed at $17.95. Now that it had arrived, the price was $19.95. And she was insisting, in a querulous sort of way, as if Miriam was trying to cheat her, that she pay only $17.95.

The phone rang. Dan, another clerk, was nearby, and Miriam, dodging, motioned him over to handle the woman while she took the phone.

To her surprise, it was Ted. His voice sounded thin. "I didn't know whether I should call you right now or not ... but ... your mother just called. Your dad fell in the bathroom and they're taking him to the hospital."

Miriam was very calm. She was taking it in, trying to figure it out. Her father had fallen in the bathroom? Her father never fell. But maybe he had slipped in the shower. And was he hurt? She felt some strange sensation of lightness, but she was also holding herself very still. It seemed important not to jump to conclusions.

"I just had a moment to talk to your mother," Ted explained, "because the paramedics were there and they were just taking him out."

Paramedics? Taking him out?

"She must have called 911," Ted said.

Out of the corner of her eye, Miriam saw Dan dealing with the difficult customer. The world around her was still there. But all her attention was focused on Ted's voice, trying to hear what had happened, what it *meant*.

Fallen in the bathroom. Paramedics. Hospital.

"Miriam," Ted said, "it looks as if he collapsed. He might have had a heart attack. It doesn't look good. Maybe you should come home."

It wasn't obvious to Miriam what she should do.

"We won't know anything for a while," Ted said.

Miriam was very calm. She hung up the phone. She tried to think what to do. Should she go home now or not? Maybe he had just fallen in the bathroom. Maybe he'd be home by that night. He wasn't the kind to get hurt. She started downstairs. She was considering not telling anyone at the bookstore about the phone call. She would go right on selling books, as if nothing had happened. Wouldn't it then be, in some way, that nothing *had* happened?

Before she could get to the stairs, a customer grabbed her. She wanted to find a book with a certain poem in it by Edna St. Vincent Millay. Miriam led her to the poetry section and looked with her through a few anthologies. She tried to find Edna St. Vincent Millay in the individual poets' section, but she couldn't think whether her last name would begin with S, V, or M. Miriam felt very confused about that.

Finally she found the *Collected Poems*. She handed it over.

As soon as she got downstairs, the phone was ringing and ringing. Out of habit she picked it up. A customer wanted to know if a book he had ordered had come in. Miriam went back upstairs to the special-order shelf, but she couldn't remember what book he had mentioned, or his name. She was kneeling by the special-order books, but she couldn't remember what she was looking for. Dan was looking at her. She looked up at him.

"I just got a phone call that my father has collapsed," she said, "and they're taking him to the hospital." Her hands started to shake. They were shaking in front of her, trying to find the book the name of which she had forgotten.

It was saying those words—*my father, collapse, hospital*—that did it. Once they were loosed, she couldn't get them back. She couldn't stop them.

Dan was full of concern. Didn't she want to go home? Miriam asked him to pick up line two and help the customer who was waiting.

Five, maybe ten minutes had passed.

Then she was in her car, driving home. She was crying, but at the same time, her mind was working quietly, efficiently. She was thinking of what she needed to do if she was going to South Carolina. When she pulled into the garage, Ted was there. When he saw Miriam, he burst into tears. Miriam was surprised. She had never seen him cry that way.

"Your Uncle Perry will be the one to call," Ted told her in the house. Miriam got her calendar, she asked Ted to call the airlines to find out about flights. She made a list of names and phone numbers of appointments and commitments that would have to be canceled. She would leave the list with a friend if she had to.

They were sitting at the dining room table when the phone rang. Uncle Perry cleared his throat, he gathered himself. "Miriam," he said into her ear, "he didn't make it."

"He didn't," Miriam repeated dully.

Her uncle, a retired doctor, related how he had met the ambulance at the hospital, how they had worked on her father, how they weren't able to save him. He had never had any heart trouble, but it was that sudden thing. The heart stops. Stops. He and Miriam's mother had gone in and viewed the body, and now they were home. Not an hour had passed.

Miriam asked to speak to her mother. "He was just fine," her mother said in a perplexed voice. "We had had lunch and were getting ready to take some letters to the post office. He said 'I have a little headache and I'm out of aspirin.' I gave him a Tylenol to take. He went into the bathroom to get ready and five minutes later, when I called to him, he didn't answer. I found him stretched out on the floor. I tried to revive him with a wet washcloth. I put a pillow under his head. But I couldn't find a pulse. I called 9ll. I didn't waste any time."

Miriam told her mother she wasn't sure she could get a flight out that afternoon. But two hours later, she and Ted were on a plane to Greenville.

She was flying to Greenville because her father had died, just as she had always known he would, and never for a minute believed. She had first started fearing her father's death when she was about fourteen. She would get up at night and stand in the doorway of her parents' bedroom to make sure he was still breathing. He was forty-five when Miriam was born, and in school she had come to understand that he was an "old" father. He didn't seem old in any way, but still, she was afraid she'd lose him before she was ready. She was forty-three now, and he would have been eighty-eight on September 17, fifteen days after he died. And while it was true that she was still not ready to lose him, and never would have been, she was grateful that she had had as long as she did to grow up before he died. It was only in the last year or two that Miriam had felt her own maturity somewhat in place.

She felt composed in a numb sort of way, aware of everything around her and yet at a remove. Her job now was to get to Greenville, and all her energy was directed toward that goal. It seemed important to get there as soon as possible, important that Miriam be there that first night to help her mother turn down the covers of the antique oak bed, the bed her father would inhabit no more, after fifty-eight years of marriage.

Miriam and Ted were sleeping in an upstairs bedroom and when Miriam turned on the light in the bathroom that first night home, the radio came on. It was an old-ies station, rock 'n' roll. Miriam stood transfixed in the bathroom, feeling her father's presence and, for the first time, his absence. He was the one who had rigged up the radio to turn on with the light. When he shaved in this bathroom, he wanted the radio on. More than anything else, radios bespoke her father. During her growing up, he had had a radio and TV store on North Main Street. Their house had always been full of radios and TVs.

It was just like her father to have that radio on. When her folks would visit them up North, it was always a joke between Miriam and Ted about how her father would want a radio or TV on the whole time. Once they took her parents to some fancy townhouses on the North Shore, which had no radios or TVs, and her father had with-drawal symptoms. Was she making it up to say he went out to the car to listen to the radio?

At any rate, when the radio burst on in the bathroom, with so much volume, it was her father all the way and it broke Miriam's heart. She went crying to Ted in the bed-room, and she was laughing, too, for her father had been something of a character. She knew she was in for a hard time then, because she needed to turn that radio off and she knew that when she did … Well. Her father would never be there to turn it on again.

Miriam cried and cried. The radio played and played. I can't turn it off, she wept to Ted, I just can't. I can't. But she wanted to.

You don't have to, Ted soothed. You can always turn it back on.

She knew. She knew. But she was beginning to know something else. Her father was dead. Each moment was another moment separating her from his living, breathing self. He had been alive a few hours earlier. Nine hours ago, he was *alive*! And now. Now his hand, which she knew so well, would never again be there to turn that radio on. Not after Miriam turned it off.

She turned it off.

The next morning, the house was full of people. The kitchen began to fill with honey-baked ham, sliced turkey, casseroles topped with potato chips or cheddar cheese, pound cake. There was so much to do that Miriam barely had time to miss her father. She had to write an obituary, find a photograph for the newspaper, help her mother make all the decisions, and meet the mortician, a handsome man about her age who remembered buying stereos from her father as a teenager. Her Aunt Grace, Uncle Perry, cousin Henry, and Henry's wife Clarice came over, and they all sat down to a big Southern lunch. Only once or twice did Miriam look up to see where her father should be sitting at the head of the table, the place he always sat.

At the mortuary that afternoon, Miriam, her mother, and Ted looked over the caskets. They were all in a showroom, as cars might be, and they had discreet cards in them with the important information, the cost. There were Rolls-Royce caskets of shiny dark mahogany, Cadillac caskets of highly burnished metal, and even a few Chevrolets and Mercuries, though nothing approaching a Toyota. Miriam noticed a huge object that turned out to be a vault and learned that, not only did one need a casket, one needed something to put the casket in.

Ted pulled her aside at some point and asked if anybody had considered cremation. Miriam was aware of that option herself, but she doubted that her mother would go for it. It might seem too Northern a thing, and Miriam was sure her mother was going to bury her father according to some internal idea, one that didn't need to be articulated. Miriam didn't know how to bury the dead, and if her mother did, that was fine with her.

Later that afternoon, Miriam and her mother returned to the mortuary to make sure that the body was laid out properly. Miriam was afraid to see her father. But at the same time, she wanted to. She hadn't seen him since last March—six months! Maybe it would have been different if she lived in the same town, if she had seen him every few days. But now she needed to see her father's face again. She had always liked being with her father. His presence, his abiding love and complete approval of her, had made her feel welcomed in the world, buoyed up. What more could a child ask for, and she was still her father's child. She still needed his love.

It didn't look like him. At first Miriam thought there had been a mistake, and of course the heart leaps, maybe it's all a mistake! *Maybe he didn't die.* But it was him, and gradually, after the initial shock, she saw that it was her father, or some form of him. His little glasses looked right, and his forehead and his white hair, which he was so proud of, but from the nose down, it might have been someone else. The mortuary had done something strange to make him look—she didn't know what. For one thing, his mouth was shut. That seemed odd, for him. He had on his best dark suit and a tie Miriam had given him, and one hand was laid across his middle, rather formally. It was his hand. Miriam could see that. That she knew. She knew those hands, and they were his, and nothing the mortuary did could change them. They were her father's hands, and they were dead. They would never rise again in all that animation that was his, all that joy. All that caring, all that tending, all that fixing, all that doing. All that love.

Miriam wanted more than anything else to go back to the mortuary alone and spend time with her father. In that confused and hectic time, this need rose like a mountain out of the mist, vivid and undeniable. There were so many people around, there was so much going on—*but where was her father?* He was missing, and if she didn't separate herself from everything else, if only for a little while, she would lose him in the commotion. She told her mother of her need.

Arrangements had to be made. It wasn't easy. Her mother needed her car to go to the beauty parlor, to get her hair done before the funeral the next day. Miriam's sister and her husband were driving down from Virginia, and Miriam's mother thought Miriam should be there when they got in. Her father's old gold Plymouth station wagon was a dubious means of transportation. Mostly it sat in the backyard like an old horse put out to pasture. Ted and her mother were afraid for Miriam to drive it to the mortuary. But Miriam had to go, that much was clear.

The station wagon drove like a boat, but it carried

Miriam all the way across town. She went into the room where her father lay, and she shut the door behind her.

II

When Miriam got back to Minnesota after the funeral, fall was in the air. She had been gone two weeks and she couldn't remember where she had left off exactly or what she had to do. But it was all waiting for her. Right away she had to start teaching and working at the bookstore, where the bestseller was a little book called *Meditations for Women Who Do Too Much*. And of course there was the book she was writing, which lay beached on her desk, out of water, stranded, dying from lack of attention.

Miriam started right in on everything. It was her life, after all; she had no choice but to live it. When people asked her how she was doing, she wasn't sure what to say. Friends kept telling her what a big thing it was, how difficult to lose a parent, and she worried if it was big enough for her. How big was it supposed to be, and how did such a loss manifest itself? She had expected to be demolished somehow, but she was coping very well. In fact, she was doing so well that she sometimes had to remind herself that her father had died. Still, her brow felt contracted, as if in concentration.

It was several weeks before she found time to walk around Lake Harriet, bundled up against a sharp wind that splashed waves high up on the north shore. The water had taken on a steely color. She could not imagine ever swimming in it. She thought back to that last summer day when she had gone swimming, and a feeling of incomprehension came over her. Overhead, Canadian geese were winging their way south in formation. There was something in their cries that stopped her in her tracks. She looked up. She shook her head. She couldn't answer.

It was just that she was so busy! She was always rushing here and there, trying to do so much, like everyone else. But then one day she wore her blouse wrong side out, and not long after that, at the grocery store when the young man asked her "plastic or paper," she said paper, and when he asked her "carry out or drive up," she said drive up. When she pulled into her garage at home, she saw the number they had given her there on the front seat. She had forgotten the groceries. But those were the kind of things she might have done before her father died, she told herself. She always had a lot on her mind, only now she had more.

Her mother had wanted Miriam and Ted to have something of Miriam's father's, so Miriam had taken his wristwatch, which had stopped working, and which she kept now in a change purse in her desk drawer. She was not able to take it out. Ted had gotten her father's little pocket knife, which her father had owned for maybe fifty years. It was always with him, either on his dresser top at night or in his pocket during the day. Her father was handy and she had seen him use it to repair rabbit ears on the TV, open a stuck sardine can, cut twine for mailing a package, or do any of the innumerable other things her father did to repair the world. Ted was glad to have it. It was a pretty little knife, ivory with streaks of gold, small, with a good feel in the hand.

Ted had it down at the dock with him the day he took the sailboat out for the winter. As he was trimming a tattered telltale, the pocket knife leaped from his hands and jumped into the water. Miriam could only stare at him in amazement when he told her. He felt so miserable about losing it, but Miriam couldn't help saying something along the lines of how her father had owned that knife for fifty years and Ted couldn't hold on to it for ten minutes. She regarded him across a great divide: *His* father hadn't died.

After that, she often thought about the knife. She couldn't get it out of her mind. How she wished to have it back! It was always leaping like a little silvery fish, leaping into the dark water, and what she couldn't get around was that it was gone. Gone!

Even though it was getting so cold, she circled Lake Harriet nearly every day, going round and round. She stared at the lake in a new way. Now it contained her father's little knife. How was it, she wondered, that her father's pocket knife had traveled all the way from South Carolina to jump into Lake Harriet a few blocks from her house in Minneapolis? The lake, looking particularly gray and remote, offered no answers.

In November the lake began to freeze. It started with crystals around the edges, then thin panes of ice spread out over the surface, which children threw sticks and rocks onto while they could still break through. One day the temperature plunged sharply and Miriam hurried down to find the lake freezing solid. It was happening and nothing could stop it.

As she walked around the lake, her face burning with cold, the freezing sheets of ice pitched high, thin notes like a tuning fork. She had read somewhere that tuning forks had a mysterious quality. If you held up several of them in a room and struck only one, the others would sound as well, absorbing vibrations through the air, answering in kind. Miriam felt the sounds coming off the lake reverberating in her, and something in her answered back in that high, keening tone: *Gone! Gone!*

• • •

She had meant to get her bulbs into the ground well before it froze, but she was very late this year. Thus she found herself on her knees one frigid day, the earth cold and hard, brown paper sacks of tulip and daffodil bulbs by her side, wearing her old green garden gloves and spading holes into which she sprinkled bone meal. As she set the last bulb into the ground and covered it, suddenly she began to weep. Her father had loved gardening. He was always growing something. His old metal watering can came into her mind, and the strips of white undershirt he had used to tie his heavy tomato vines to stakes. He was wearing a white undershirt when he died; the paramedics had cut it open to get to his heart. She wept into her garden gloves, smearing her face with dirt. *Her father was gone! She would never see him again!* How was this possible? It was not possible. How could she stand it? She could not stand it. She got creakily to her feet. She went in the house and washed her face.

It began to snow in December. At first there were just a few light dustings, against which the earth battled back. But then it began in earnest, seriously, with great determination. Standing at the window, watching the snow swirl and float out of the sky, vanishing the familiar world, Miriam felt despair. It was as if she came from a country where it never snowed; how she longed to return to that green land! Of course she knew snow, she had lived in Minnesota for a long time, she liked snow, she even liked winter, sort of, but now it weighed her down. It made her long for sleep.

One wintry afternoon she was driving home from her class at the university, listening to the local public radio station. It was snowing and Miriam was afraid to drive in snow, but she pushed on, just as everyone around her on the freeway was doing. She tried to concentrate on Michael Friezen's voice. Though she had never met him, she was very fond of him; she often thought of him as her best friend, at least when she had the radio on. She loved how he read poetry, how he so appreciated the seasons and, most of all, how he loved music. Today's selections, he began, were in honor of the snow, which was falling so gently, so softly, covering everything over, falling—and here he quoted Joyce—"upon all the living and the dead."

He had chosen Strauss's *Four Last Songs* to begin the afternoon's program. The songs, he explained, expressed serene confidence in eternity and immortality. "In them," he said deeply, "the voice is allowed to soar within an exceptionally wide compass, giving the impression of an instrument with vocal qualities."

Before Miriam was ready, the music began. The first chords struck several slow funereal notes, against which broke a clear, pure soprano, as if the human heart had been translated into sound. This voice lifted higher and higher, seeking to escape the bounds of earth, taking with it all grief, all sorrow, and it tore Miriam from her moorings, lifting her, too. She was weeping. She was weeping so much, in fact, that she needed to pull off the freeway. She maneuvered her way out of the speeding traffic, sliding through the snow at forty miles per hour, and stopped. She stopped. Cars zoomed past her; she put her face in her hands and wept. *Her father was gone. She would never see him again.* This simple truth rose up in her. It opened up in her, it opened her up. An inner life, which she was hardly aware of but which nevertheless was going about its work, had chosen this moment to make itself known. Most of the time she skimmed along the surface, trying to keep head above water. But now she sensed fathoms. She sounded the depths.

• • •

Miriam and Ted flew to South Carolina to be with her mother for the first Christmas. It shocked Miriam to see how her mother had aged since her father's death. For many years he had been the old one; now her mother's turn had arrived. She would be seventy-nine in January. There were all the questions of her mother's old age: Could she continue to live alone; and if not, where should she live? And how to fix the glove compartment door of her old Buick, which kept falling open, which Miriam's father would have fixed.

Walking across the uneven winter grass at the cemetery, holding onto her mother's arm to keep her from falling, Miriam hardly thought of her father at all. She was thinking instead of how old and shaky her mother had become, of whether they should get her a microwave and if she could master it, and of the approaching day when Miriam would fly away, again.

When Miriam returned to Minnesota in January, she looked around in surprise. Having gotten through fall and the holidays, she had expected to be let off the hook. But her father was still dead. He was going to go right on being dead forever.

Now began the days of deepest winter: four degrees below zero; ten below. The world was monochromatic, stark, shut down. She thought back to that summer day; she had been innocent then, as green as a leaf. It was harder to make herself go down to the lake now. But still she went. It lay so still and frozen. Impossible to believe it could ever be the inviting blue of summer. Everything was cold. Miriam was cold. She turned down invitations when she could. The weather was as good an excuse as any; no one much liked to go out, especially in the dark, cold night. Now was winter: solitude, privacy, silence, snow.

She quit her job at the bookstore. She needed the money, but she couldn't afford to make it. She spent her days making soup: black bean, vegetable beef. She sat in a rocker for hours, listening to music: Beethoven's *Moonlight Sonata*, Brahms' sublimely beautiful choral work of lamentation, *Nänie*, Chopin's *Nocturne in E Flat Major*. Outside the snow glittered in the cold, crystalline air. When she taught, her students moved her: their beauty, their youth. She took long baths, fragrant with oils, pungent with salts. She was silent and still, watching the birds at the feeder.

Deep one night she dreamed of her father. He wasn't old, as she had last known him in life, or even young, but rather no age at all—just himself, outside of time. They were in the garden, planting shrubs. He had on his garden gloves, old soft ones of cotton ticking. How happy she was to see him! What comfort in being with him again. Miriam knew that she was dreaming. She knew that he wouldn't be staying. But for now they were in the garden, planting green things.

Miriam awoke. She went to stand at the window. Below, the garden was covered with snow, a dark radiance in the night. Under its glow, flowers and bulbs were sleeping through this long winter's night.

Miriam went in for a massage. The masseuse was an ex-nun named Joan with arms like a fullback. She had Miriam undress completely in the bathroom of her suburban ranch house and lie face down on a massage table in an extra bedroom that had been converted into a quasi-

New Age den. Joan and Miriam made small talk at first, but then they both fell silent. It felt good to Miriam to have her back massaged with such power. All her muscles, knotted from the long, cold winter, were being smoothed out under the force of Joan's strong hands.

Outside the wind chill was minus forty-four degrees; but inside, Miriam, feeling naked and small, was warm. She buried her face in the hole in the massage table. Every now and then Joan would stop and simply rest her hand for a moment on Miriam's back, as if Miriam were a baby and Joan were reassuring her. Miriam began to cry. The weeping rose from deep in her body, from a physical place she hadn't even known existed. It was as if Joan had released these tears from Miriam's tissues. She didn't so much think the words this time as feel them: *He's gone. Never again.* Above her Joan rested her hand lightly on Miriam's sobbing back.

"'Tis very warm winter when one's in bed,'" Ted says to Miriam. They're in bed and it is very warm.

"Who said that?" Miriam asks. He majored in English, and often surprises her with quotes.

"How would I know," he says, taking her in his arms.

"'Tis," she says, kissing him softly.

She's neglected Ted over this long winter of her father's death. It's as if she's been away, though of course she's been here all along. Still, she hasn't quite been able to notice him in some way, though she understands that he has been noticing her, watching and waiting for her all through this long, cold time.

She does notice him now, notices the pleasing smell of his neck, notices his large hands on her bare back, the way he tilts her chin to kiss her, the quickening taste of his tongue. Let's face it, lovemaking for Miriam sometimes seems just another "thing to do" on her apparently endless list. But not today. On this frosty Sunday afternoon when it's too cold to go outside, she wants only to burrow—into the house, into the bedroom, into the bed, into Ted. Though maybe he is burrowing into her. It is sometimes hard to tell.

Then there comes the moment, as they progress, when her body tenses, becomes taut, like an instrument, a stringed instrument against which a bow is being drawn, *now*, releasing one high, sweet note. And once again, Miriam is weeping. This time the weeping comes from such a deep place that Miriam can't tell if what she feels is pleasure or pain, joy or sorrow.

Ted folds her to him.

Miriam begins swimming in an indoor pool which is in a kind of glass dome. It has a running track on the floor above and is encircled by walls of windows, a lot of light flooding down on the water. She goes as often as she can. She has the time. She's slowed way down; swimming helps her do that. Maybe it's the ritual of it, how it takes over an hour to go there, undress, swim, shower, dry her hair, and all that time she isn't even thinking. She never hurries. She remembers how her father, raised in the country, liked to sit on the porch. Just sit! He might have the radio on, or he might not. He wouldn't do a thing. Just *be*. Swimming gives Miriam some of that same feeling.

Today she has the pool to herself, perhaps because of the forecast. Twelve more inches of snow, and no one wants to be out in a blizzard. But it wasn't snowing when Miriam left home, and she wanted so much to go swimming. Now she enters the water, feeling the pleasure of her crawl. Arm over arm, legs flutter kicking behind her, she moves smoothly and lightly through the blue water. She does lap after lap, as if she could never tire. Memories float through her: summer days at Table Rock Lake where she grew up swimming, her father's leaping pocketknife, sailing with Ted on his J boat. She'll swim in Lake Harriet again this summer. She'll make a point of doing so, and not just once.

She stands up. She is all alone. It is perfectly quiet. Up above, through the glass dome, she sees that it is snowing. The snow is coming down in big, beautiful flakes. Before her the water is calm and blue. She begins to walk through it, slowly, trailing her hands. She moves in slow motion, watching her fingers part the water in incandescent waves.

And now she's aware of a presence. She understands that she is being watched over, guarded. Or maybe it's only the snow. It has the feel of snow—beautiful, silvery, silent, filling the air. This is what angels are like, she thinks. And this is what snow is like. How it falls and falls, how it blesses us.

You're gone. I'll never see you again.

But this time she doesn't cry. She walks in the water, trailing her fingers, looking up at the snow.

Her Mother's Pocketbook

Actually, her mother has a number of pocketbooks, though not so many, these days, as she once had.

Miriam has only to shut her eyes to see them lined on her mother's current closet shelf, and to her they are not so much like pocketbooks as they are like people. There's the formal pink leather one, with its straight hard sides and rigid Plexiglas handles, a proper Southern lady dressed for a ladies' luncheon at the country club. There's a soft black pouchy purse from the forties, made of a felt-like material, with no supports, so that it squashes down as if it's lost its will, but with a beautiful gold bar clasp across the top that saves it from total helplessness. There's a sturdy saddlebag, middle-aged, capable of bearing much, and a silly spring thing of white, with lattice sides and two handles as skinny and pliable as young girls. And then there's the brown faux-leather one, plain and simple, which her mother uses for everyday, mostly finished, as she is, with the phantasmagoria of life.

These, however, are only the survivors. Many others have perished of late, all those purses and pocketbooks that peopled her mother's closet at home, in Greenville, South Carolina, before Linda and Miriam uprooted her this past winter to move her close to Miriam, in Minnesota. For years they had known that the time was coming, and for years their mother had resisted, not wanting to leave her own home, all those closets, a myriad of pocketbooks, not to mention everything else. Not only was the house filled with their parents' stuff, for truly it could be said that they never threw out a thing, it was also filled with Miriam's grandmother's belongings, for when her mother moved her own mother first to a one-bedroom apartment and then to the nursing home, she simply brought all her mother's material possessions, including her pocketbooks (still good!) home.

Perhaps it was the weight of all those familiar things that held them all down, that kept them from action. But how were they to move their mother, when she didn't want to go? With a shoehorn? A crowbar? A hoist and derrick, perhaps? So on and on she lived, alone after her husband's death. Gradually, over time, Linda and Miriam noticed that their mother was losing, if not her mind, then certainly her memory. Over long distance they called their mother, Miriam from Minnesota, Linda from Virginia, and those conversations would make them think, *We've got to do something, we've got to make a move.*

But once they were home, there in their parents' comfortable old den, with the big Clemson tiger picture over her mother's La-Z-Boy rocker, the old Magnavox console TV as immovable as a boulder before them, it didn't seem that remembering who had been there that day, or what she had had for dinner, was that big a deal. And as their mother herself said, *Does it matter that I can't remember those things?* It did and it didn't.

Then in October, when Miriam was in Greenville, she suddenly understood that they had to move their mother. They could not go on another day, though of course they had to. Formerly, Miriam had passed off the expression "crystal clear" as a cliché. But now she couldn't keep those words from her own lips; she tasted them again and again. Having wrung her hands for years over this decision, now she marveled at her own certainty. Only a few times in her life has Miriam been so sure of what to do, and always such knowledge has been accompanied by a surprising, satisfying sense of peace. Crystal clear, for such understanding is like crystal, capturing and giving off light, without the usual muddiness of anxiety, ambivalence, and fear.

And Miriam knew more. She knew that she wanted to move her mother near to her. Her mother, sister, and Miriam had always assumed that when the time came, Mother would move to Virginia, to be near Linda. None of them could imagine moving her to Minnesota. No one, especially a lifelong Southerner, moves to Minnesota in old age. It's just the opposite: Everyone who can moves *out* of Minnesota in old age. But now Miriam realized that she was furious, seriously, deeply mad that something like weather could keep her from her mother. She had been away from her for so long, and now she needed to be near her. To take care of her. To see her through to the end.

Miriam didn't know how her mother would react to her certainty that the time had finally come to move. Only two weeks before Miriam's October visit, Linda had been to see their mother and had talked to her about moving. Their mother had put up a fierce battle, saying hotly to Linda, "You'll have to carry me out of here feet first."

But she had fallen (again) since Linda had been there, and was complaining of pain in her rib cage. Miriam took her to her doctor, Jimmy Jones, who had been their neighbor on Paris Mountain, a skinny red-haired kid two or three years younger than Miriam. "He used to play in our creek," was how her mother described him. Indeed, she had a broken rib, and then there was the problem with dizziness, which Miriam thought might be from not eating regularly. She had help, Frances, for four hours three times a week, but otherwise she was on her own. She could barely walk, something that had happened over time, gradually, incrementally, helped along by her occasional falls. She wore a lifeline, but she couldn't remember what it was for, so every time she fell, she'd crawl to the phone and dial 911.

Clearly, it was time. Miriam presented it to her mother as such. *The time has come.* Miriam told her that she wanted her to move to Minneapolis. She and Linda would take care of everything. And her mother agreed. She had a realistic streak that Miriam had always counted on. She certainly had her emotions—her temper, her pride, her sorrow—but always she had been able to face up to what actually *is*.

She knew, perhaps better than anyone, that she could no longer take care of herself. Her memory had lost its magnetic charge. She'd say she hadn't talked to Linda in three or four weeks, when they had spoken on Sunday. She couldn't remember how much or when to take her medication, swallowing a pill whenever she felt dizzy or her heartbeat was rapid. Many of her friends had died, or were in no condition to come see her. "I can't think for myself anymore," she said, "so you and Linda will have to think for me."

Miriam wasn't sure how Linda would feel about their mother moving to Minnesota. For all Miriam knew, Linda had to have their mother, too. They discussed the matter in terms of logic. Linda had a full-time government job; Miriam taught writing and had more time to take care of Mother; people mostly survived Minnesota winters. Linda acquiesced so quickly and easily that Miriam had the uneasy sense that she'd been had. But again she felt that certainty, that clear, crystal light.

• • •

Back in Minnesota, Miriam went into action. She was teaching, but during every free moment she looked into places to move her mother. She began to get serious about money, her mother's money, how much was there, how much might the house bring. On her end, Linda also got busy. They were a perfect team, a complementary division of labor. Linda contacted a real estate agent, flew to Greenville and began to throw out huge amounts of the stuff that had held so much of their parents' lives. It was the opposite of an archeological dig. Instead of unearthing and preserving the past, she was destroying a lost world, layer by layer.

And there were a lot of layers. Linda started with the easy, throwaway stuff no one felt particularly sentimental about. Huge black garbage bags of it sat on the curb, where strangers went through it. Then she progressed deeper and deeper, into the painful nerve centers. Linda, tougher in some ways (though not in others) than Miriam, was the right one to do it.

Miriam hid out in Minneapolis during the slaughter, occupying herself with the future, preparing a new home for her mother. She was filled with an unfamiliar emotion, which might have been ecstasy but could also have been shock. She couldn't believe that they were selling the house, that she was moving her mother to Minnesota, that they were leaving Greenville, which, twenty-plus years to the contrary, Miriam still considered home.

Miriam was teaching an interim course during the month of January, and it was cold. So cold, in fact, that her mother's furniture, which Linda shipped to Minnesota in a Mayflower van, sat in Hudson, Wisconsin, an hour out of the Twin Cities, for five days when the temperature did not rise above twenty degrees below zero, dipping down at night to thirty or forty degrees below. The diesel engine in the truck wouldn't start.

Miriam had thought that her mother's furniture would arrive in time for her to unpack all the boxes and get everything just so before she flew to Greenville at the beginning of February to bring her mother back to the wonderful world that Miriam had created for her. But her mother's things got stuck in Hudson. When they were finally delivered, Miriam only had time to stuff clothes into closets and push boxes to the side, so at least there was a clear path into the apartment. The few dishes and pots and pans she did unpack burned her hands like dry ice.

Miriam turned in grades and flew off to South Carolina, to Greenville, where she had grown up, where her parents had lived their lives, to pull her mother up by the roots and transplant her to Minnesota, in the dead of winter. The idea was that Miriam would stay a week, they'd fly back together, and then Linda would return to the scene of the crime for the final kill. The house had sold amazingly fast, for cash. After Miriam and her mother left, an estate person would come in and sell everything that remained. Linda was taking some furniture back to Virginia, and they had shipped what her mother could use for the new apartment to Minnesota, but a lot was still left. Miriam tried halfheartedly to deal with some of it. She felt she owed it to Linda to throw something out, but she was not constitutionally suited for discarding any of her parents' lives.

Upstairs, where her mother was not able to go anymore, their father's old study contained a wall of boxed slide carousels. The carousels could be recycled, but what of the slides themselves, all those pictures Miriam's father took of their trips, the mountains on endless fall outings, the beach, years passing, Miriam and Linda growing up, the good years, the best years, back when their parents were still young and vital, never dreaming of this moment when Miriam would stand in the emptying house, trying to dispose of the bright moments that had once meant so much. She tried, she really did, throwing away "Japan" and "Italy"—her father had won trips as an RCA dealer—but she slipped out the slides of her own European trip her parents had given her as a college graduation present and some slides of holiday dinners: Christmas '65, Thanksgiving '71. She knew she'd probably never look at them. She didn't have a slide projector and this was just the sort of thing—mooning over the past—she never had time for, though she deeply desired it. The present always demanded so much that it elbowed, rather roughly, Miriam thought, the past to the side, to the back, away. She packed up a couple more boxes of things she couldn't part with and shipped them off to Minneapolis.

Then it was time to leave. They had an intentionally early plane to catch, so the morning of their departure would be swift. Her mother had told Miriam's husband, Ted, over the phone that she had expected to be weepy about leaving, but found she wasn't. Indeed, as the taxi pulled away from the house for the last time, her mother did not turn to look back, her familiar brown, faux-leather pocketbook held snugly on her lap.

Now her mother can't find her pocketbook. She calls up in a snit, basically, disgusted that she can't find it and wanting Miriam to come over and find it. She's living in the senior-citizen building ten minutes away from Miriam in Minneapolis, and she can't find her pocketbook. Miriam just groans. Lost Pocketbook Syndrome is getting to her.

The place where her mother lives is called Wedgwood Manor, a pretty name. Her mother's apartment, on the sixth floor, faces out onto the tops of trees, though now, in March, they are bare. Wedgwood Manor has "a la carte assisted-living services," which is why Miriam chose it. Meals on Wheels delivers her mother's lunch Monday through Friday. Because she can't make it to the dining room on her own memory or mobility, Wedgwood Manor brings her dinner up every night. She gets a bath once a week from Cathy, a home health aide who calls her mother "chum" and housecleaning once a week from Kate, a lovely young woman who just graduated from the small liberal arts college where Miriam teaches. Kate majored in French, is looking for a teaching job, and in the meantime cleans apartments. But the real "assisted living" comes from Miriam. It seems that is all she is doing these days: assisting her mother with living.

Like today, when her mother can't find her pocketbook.

"Isn't it hanging on the big pink chair in your bedroom?" Miriam asks over the phone.

"It's not there," her mother says peevishly. "I've looked everywhere! It's not here!"

Her mother is growing crankier and more agitated by the minute. This isn't the first time she's misplaced her pocketbook. The last time she had hidden it under a handmade quilt in her cedar chest. It took Miriam a long time to find it. Since then, she's tried to train her mother to hang it on the pink chair. "Maybe it's in the cedar chest."

"Come over here and look for it," her mother orders.

Recently, Miriam has been remembering one of the many reasons she was so eager to leave home so long ago: to get away from her mother, her imperious ways. Funny how Miriam had not exactly forgotten that, but misplaced it as an active memory.

Miriam stops herself from saying her mother doesn't really need her pocketbook. At least not right now, today, this minute. Miriam has taken all her credit cards out, along with her insurance, Medicare, and Senior Gold cards. There's not much money in the pocketbook, a few dollars, and Miriam keeps her checkbook now. She shuts her eyes and sees her mother's little brown pocketbook so clearly, the one her mother always wants to take if they go out somewhere. It has a long, thin shoulder strap and one snap to hold it closed. It's lightweight, because there is so little in it. Just her mother's wallet and driving license, though she doesn't drive anymore, her social security card, her rain bonnet, a linen handkerchief, a few peppermints. They never go anywhere without her mother wanting to take this bag, and then she can never remember if they have brought it. "Do you have my pocketbook?" she'll ask several times during any outing. Several, as in many.

Miriam, wanting to be kind, patient, a fountain of forbearance, will find herself gritting her teeth, grimacing, exasperated, struggling not to snap at her mother. She's always struggling these days, struggling with her mother, her mother's walker, her own purse, their coats, and her mother's damn pocketbook, which her mother can't carry herself while pushing her walker. The pocketbook is always in the way, falling off Miriam's shoulder or bumping into something as Miriam tries to maneuver her mother through a door. And then there's her mother's inability to remember, five seconds after Miriam has reassured her, that yes, she has it. *Do you have my pocketbook? Did I bring a pocketbook? Where's my pocketbook?*

But today Miriam doesn't have the pocketbook, and her mother is over there alone in the apartment with a missing person, so to speak. Miriam must go over. Her mother won't rest until it is found, and Miriam knows enough to know her mother can't find it herself. In many ways, her once-formidable mother is helpless. She will never be able to remember where her pocketbook is, and though she will search, she will not be able to find it.

Miriam doesn't know why. Something is terribly wrong in her mother's brain. Something has shorted out her short-term memory. It is like a fuse that has blown, so that part of the house is dark while the rest is brightly lit. It isn't as if she can't remember anything. She certainly knows who she is, and who Miriam is, but anything new, anything she has to learn, doesn't stick. It blows straight through, as if her mother's memory were a barbed-wire fence on the prairie that might catch a stray piece of paper that sticks for a moment, and is gone in the next, leaving no trace.

Miriam had imagined a certain life for her mother in Minneapolis, at Wedgwood Manor: making friends, eating in the dining room in the evenings, playing bingo in the party room. But her mother can't go to the dining room, because she can't ride the elevator by herself. (Miriam was shocked to learn that her mother's ability to master the elevator was about the equivalent of Miriam's ability to master quantum physics.) She can't walk the long hall to the dining room, she can't remember which floor she lives on or which apartment. She can't remember anything! She eats every meal alone in her apartment. Miriam goes over as often as she can, three, four, five times a week. She calls her mother at least three times a day, in the morning (to see if she has survived the night), at lunch (to see if Meals on Wheels has arrived), and in the evening (to make sure she hasn't fallen that afternoon). Miriam has seriously— seriously!—overestimated her mother's ability to live by herself, care for herself. Miriam is her lifeline. How could she have known? It wouldn't have made any difference.

Now Miriam goes over and finds her mother's pocketbook. It's hanging with a dress on a hanger in the closet, which is crammed with all her mother's many clothes. Some of them are really beautiful, really fine. Things twenty-five, thirty years old, and better made than anything one can buy today. She fixes her mother tea and cinnamon toast, as if her mother is a child. Her mother, sitting at the small dining room table (they shipped up Miriam's grandmother's drop-leaf table), seems content, dreamy, looking out the window at the bare trees. When Miriam leaves, her mother stands at that window, looking down into the parking lot where Miriam is getting into her car. She turns and sees her mother, who always watches her leave like this. Always waves. Her mother reminds Miriam of a dog at the window, left home alone when everyone else goes off to work. Alone, alone-oh.

Miriam decides to have an open house for her mother and invite the women on the hall. At least most of them are women. People are friendly when she sees them in the elevator. But most of the time her mother's hall is quiet and deserted. No one in sight. It takes Miriam to bustle into her mother's apartment, bringing in life, energy, movement. To tell the truth, it's exhausting, living for two. So maybe friends are the answer, or at least part of the answer.

They used to have such lovely parties in Greenville. Her mother was a typical 1950s housewife, giving bridge-party luncheons, going to teas, hosting a big open house on Christmas Eve every year. Miriam makes little invitations and slips them under all the doors on the hall: Sunday, 2-4, please come. She prepares a ridiculous amount of food: a pound cake, strawberries, shrimp dip and crackers, cheese biscuits, spicy nuts, the kind of things they used to have at parties. She uses a white linen tablecloth and some of her mother's Wedgwood china and silver. Candles, flowers. Four or five people come. Conversation is a bit strained. She and her mother are overdressed, compared to the ladies in their sweat suits and tennis shoes. Miriam makes conversation for her mother, overly animated, trying too hard. Her mother reminds her of an adolescent girl, with Miriam as her pushy mother, trying to make her popular. She desperately wants some of these women to visit her mother sometimes. Her mother has proved recalcitrant, in Miriam's opinion, in terms of making friends here. She has some stubborn sense of who she is and who "her kind" of people are. When so much else has gone, why can't this kind of snobbishness go, the feeling that she's too good for some people? She's hopelessly Southern compared to most of the women in the building, who all seem to come from North Dakota and be tougher, like prairie grass, less spoiled than her mother. Most of them have worked all their lives; several have never been married. Her mother is cautious about making friends, wary of getting stuck with someone she can't get rid of. She's always been smart. But Miriam feels desperate, she wants more people in her mother's life, so she doesn't have to feel guilty when she's not there.

Miriam has an insight: She needs to go over to her mother's nearly every day (five out of seven, say), not because of her mother's need (though that is certainly there), but because of her own. She can't distinguish her mother's need from her own, they run together so. On Thursday, for example, when she didn't go over to her mother's, she noticed in herself, along with a certain relief and freedom, a sense of loneliness or grief, even. And she felt depressed. She thinks maybe her mother is depressed, being alone all day. But then, on further examination, she realizes this is probably a projection. Her mother expresses no depression, nor does Miriam see any evidence of it. Her mother is used to being alone—but this in itself depresses Miriam, who wants her mother to have a good time always, as if that were possible. Especially at eighty-five.

Of course the fact that she didn't go over on Thursday doesn't mean that she didn't tend to her mother. She took the opportunity to go to the mall and buy her mother some new stockings. Her mother wears hose that attach to garters, a style Miriam associates with sexiness. Indeed, on the packages the model's legs look quite sexy, with the hose attached to mid-thigh garters. Strong, young, sexy legs. Unlike her mother's legs, bowed and covered with strange discolorations and spots, splotches, blotches, red places, a dermatologist's field day.

When Miriam quizzed her mother about what kind of stockings to buy, her mother said she always got two boxes. Miriam finds herself repeating this request to the young saleswoman at Dayton's. Even as she says it, a lost world comes back to her, of Ivy's in Greenville and the way stockings, good stockings, used to come in boxes. Stockings don't come in boxes anymore, and Miriam feels slightly mortified, like an old person herself, totally out of it. Often, transacting business for her mother—such as buying Depends—she'll make sure that the salesperson knows she is buying them for her mother. She'd like to distance herself from Metamucil, but truth be told, she sometimes takes it herself now in middle age.

Miriam buys two packages of stockings that will attach to her mother's garters. Her mother always, always wears a girdle. She uses it, it seems, to hold herself up, like a band of extra muscles and bone, now that her own spine has literally let her down. She struggles with this elastic encasement every time she goes to the bathroom, looking little and frail until she pulls it down. Then her flesh, white and bloated, seems to balloon out. Miriam has to help her pull the girdle back up, over nylon undies, size 8, struggling to stuff the sticky warm flesh back into its too-small cage.

When Miriam comes out of the mall with the new stockings, she feels disoriented. She can't remember where exactly she parked the car. She knows she came in on the second floor of Dayton's. She paid special attention when she entered through the men's department, even staring at some men's jackets to fix them in her mind, so that she could exit through the correct door and find the car. But she has come out a different door in the men's department. Now she has no idea if her car is in this lot or not. The area looks strangely, anonymously familiar. But there aren't that many cars, and Miriam can't see her Toyota, even when she walks down a row or two. She looks across the street to see what buildings are there, to try to orient herself. But even that is confusing. Is that France Ave or 66th Street? She can't tell.

Finally she goes back in Dayton's, backtracking to come out the same door she went in. She realizes, when she exits, that she was in the Alligator lot previously, instead of Tiger. She feels shaken. So this is what old age must feel like. Heck, it's what middle age feels like. This disorientation, even fear. It was only practice fear, in that she was still pretty much in control of the situation. But what would it be like to feel really lost, not to have enough of your mind to guide you? No wonder her mother stays in her apartment.

• • •

Often her mother is dizzy. Miriam wants to fix it. Dizzy threatens everything: her dream that she can take care of her mother, that her mother can live out a few more years, or even months, without going into a nursing home They lurch from mini-crisis to mini-crisis, from phone call to phone call, her mother calling to say she's dizzy, which is Miriam's cue to haul ass over there. Once her mother called and Miriam said, basically, *Well, I don't know what to do about it*, meaning you're dizzy and I can't fix it, so I don't think I'll rush right over. To which her mother said, "Well, you think about it, Miriam," and hung up. At which point Miriam rose from her desk as if pulled by a rope, and fifteen minutes later was over at her mother's, ministering.

Miriam has taken her mother to a gerontologist about the dizziness. He didn't have any magic answers. Almost as an afterthought, he recommended Meclazine, an over-the-counter motion-sickness drug. Now, whenever her mother is dizzy, Miriam gives her two or three Meclazines, like sugar pills, and feeds her, and gradually her mother gets over the dizziness.

Still, Miriam wants more. She wants something done, if not for her mother, for herself. She is the "sole caregiver," often looking around to find those other siblings in town who can spell her, but they don't exist. There is only her sister, Linda, in Virginia. Miriam notices that she's beginning to regard Linda with a certain unfair bitterness, thinking of her as a babe in the woods, someone who doesn't know shit about what it means to be solely, totally, always responsible for their aging mother!

Whose idea was it, anyway, to move their mother to Minnesota, so that Miriam would have to take care of her all the time!

Oh.

Right.

Finally, in her infinite desire to fix things, Miriam takes her mother to a neurologist, a Dr. Heiring. While they're waiting, Miriam tells her mother for the umpteenth time that they're going to a neurologist, to see if she can help her mother's dizziness. Her mother, for the umpteenth time, asks where they heard of this doctor and what the neurologist's name is. When Miriam tells her, her mother makes a little joke: "So we're hiring Dr. Heiring."

Miriam laughs. Her mother is still sharp. She actually has a sense of humor, something about her Miriam has always enjoyed. Not that her mother is exactly a fun person. But Miriam has to hand it to her, at least occasionally. She is often impressed by her mother's strong will, which is different, it turns out, from strength. She has a kind of wry intelligence about her that Miriam appreciates and often marvels at. Her mother is not well educated, having only gone to junior college. She often seems dumb as a stone to Miriam, especially now that her brain is damaged in some way. But in another way, her mother is really smart, animal smart maybe, and Miriam often has to admit that her mother is right, even when they're disagreeing. It's certainly aggravating for sure, because sometimes her mother's being right thwarts some wish or desire on Miriam's part.

A young woman comes into the waiting area and helps Miriam's mother into a wheelchair. It's only when she introduces herself that Miriam realizes she's the doctor. So young and so serious, a neurologist, for Pete's sake. Miriam, approaching fifty, feels passed by by life. She's not a neurologist and never will be. Not that she wants to be, but still. She has banked on youth for so long, on future possibilities, that it is a shock to discover herself firmly middle-aged. Losing her own memory, from what it appears. Just last night, for hardly the first time, she wanted to say a word—"react"—in conversation. It had taken one, two beats to find it in her mental computer. No big thing, really, but still. It never used to happen. Everyone is joking about it, all her aging friends. But is it really funny? No.

Why don't these doctors ever read the reports from other doctors that they receive, by fax, before a consultation! Why, for instance, doesn't Dr. Heiring know when her mother had a CAT scan? Why does she ask Miriam, who wants to screech, *Isn't it there in her records?* Miriam doesn't know herself. She wasn't there. It was several years ago, before she moved her mother to Minnesota. Miriam can't even remember (God!) if she had the CAT scan because of the dizziness, or what. It's all a blur. She does know, from her mother's Minneapolis gerontologist, that the CAT scan didn't offer a good view of the back of the brain, where he suspected Miriam's mother had suffered a deep stroke. When he said that at their first visit, a lot had fallen into place. No one had ever suggested a stroke, back in Greenville. Miriam suspected that maybe it had seemed impolite. Their internist there, the neighbor boy who had grown up to become a doctor, had combined professionalism with a certain boyish deference, along with his Southern manners. He had never said anything about a stroke, and he certainly never used the "A" word.

It was this new, Minneapolis gerontologist who had, simply by holding one finger up in front of her mother's face and moving it this way and that, enlightened Miriam to the fact that in some places, her mother saw double. That explained why she closed one eye when she read; Miriam had attributed that to a bad prescription in her glasses. He also told them that her mother's walking problems and her lack of balance—all those falls—had to do with this stroke business in the back of her brain. Miriam had thought it was just arthritis.

The girl-neurologist has nothing new to offer Miriam's mother. Meclazine, that's about it, something they could have gotten from the druggist. Miriam feels exhausted. She feels mystified, frustrated, and frightened. What is she going to do about her mother? How can they go on?

Miriam decides to teach a memoir course at Wedgwood Manor. The course will be a place where her mother can meet other people in the building, have "something to do," make friends. Besides, it might be fun. Miriam figures she might learn about her mother's background. How she wishes her mother would write about her childhood, her girlhood, her parents, her grandparents. All the things they never get very far in talking about.

But her mother is too dizzy to go to the first meeting. And indeed, she never attends a single one of the sessions, always making an excuse or simply refusing, putting her foot down, as she is prone to do. At first Miriam is irked. She feels like a captive audience for the six old women in the course, who don't, it turns out, really want to write so much as they want to talk. To tell. They tell endlessly about their pasts, and Miriam feels bored and aggravated that she has to sit there and listen. But gradually she relaxes and lets go of her own expectations for the course. So what if they can only write a little, a paragraph or a page a week, or nothing at all? It *is* fun to hear their stories, as Miriam gets to know them. It's good for them to tell. So they aren't going to be writers; they still want to pass on some of their pasts to their children, grandchildren, and other relatives. Miriam gives them assignments, suggestions: Write about the house where you grew up; describe a grandparent. One day she is struck that they all say, spontaneously, that they miss their mothers. They're seventy-five, eighty, eighty-five years old, and they miss their mothers. Miriam is both surprised and not surprised.

Their mothers live on, vividly, in their memories. They tell little details about their mothers. Six floors up, Miriam's own mother dozes in her La-Z-Boy rocker.

Miriam joins a caregivers' support group. It consists of eight sessions with a social worker, who brings in guest speakers on topics such as stress management, coping with behavior problems, legal and financial considerations, nursing home placement, and community resources.

Miriam gets to know the other people attending the group, all of whom are caring for an aging relative. It's pretty depressing stuff, mainly. Miriam tells them about the time she and Ted took her mother for a ride around St. Paul, how her mother threw up in the car, and how Miriam couldn't stop laughing. Telling the group, Miriam is gratified that they all laugh too. Maybe throw-up stories are inherently funny, releasing some latent anxiety in everyone. Maybe it's relief that it wasn't you who threw up. Her mother had gotten car sick, and they had nothing, not one thing, in the car to catch it. The last thing her mother was able to say was, "Do you have a bucket?," as if they drove around with a bucket in the car. Now Miriam does. Her mother had barfed big-time into her hands and all over the dashboard of the passenger seat next to an appalled Ted. Miriam, in the back seat, started laughing and really couldn't stop. Luckily her mother took it in stride, though Miriam sensed through her tears how mystified her mother and Ted were by her behavior.

One night the guest speaker leads them through some exercises: Draw a wheel picture of your support system; use color crayons to indicate on a stick figure where you feel stress in your body. She wants the group to list things they've lost as a result of their loved one's age or disability.

People begin naming things: friends, free time, fun, time to themselves, dancing. Miriam doesn't say a thing. The social worker turns to her and asks if she wants to share.

There is a long uncomfortable moment of silence while Miriam composes herself. Finally she manages, "I wouldn't be able to do that. Just now. In public."

Miriam never knows what to expect when she goes over to her mother's apartment. Will it be a good day or bad, a good moment, or bad? But this afternoon when she arrives, her mother isn't dizzy. They sit out on her balcony, taking in the late spring afternoon. They look at the lilac bushes blooming in the alley below and at the leaves coming out on the trees. Miriam feels what she hardly ever feels anymore: that inner sense of light. Or maybe it's that she hardly ever notices it, she's so busy whirling around, trying to fix things. Things are working out. She's taking care of her mother. It's what she wants to do. It won't go on forever. Her mother is here.

And now, sitting on the balcony together, her mother says a simple and true thing: "I'm glad we could have this time together." Miriam is glad, too. In a way, it's a dream come true. It feels like a dream, sitting out on a balcony in Minnesota with her mother, looking at the tops of greening trees. They talk about old houses they've lived in, though her mother has forgotten the last one, on Cleveland Street. She refers to it, when Miriam recalls it to her, as an "afterthought," though she lived in it for eighteen years. But she does remember their house on Paris Mountain, the house they built, where Miriam grew up.

Miriam reads her the gardening section from the *Ladies Home Journal*, and then it is time to go down to dinner. Occasionally Miriam wheels her mother to the dining room on the first floor. She's bought a used wheelchair, the best purchase she's ever made. Her mother refers to going down to the dining room as "eating out." Naturally, she wants to take her pocketbook, the little brown faux-leather one, and naturally it is lost again. But Miriam finds it without too much trouble, in the bottom dresser drawer. She has learned, over these past few months, where to look for it.

Just as they are finishing dinner, a woman they've chatted with several times in the elevator comes over to their table. Though Miriam can tell her mother doesn't remember meeting her (Miriam strains to come up with her name, Fran), her mother seems happy to be recognized, known. Fran asks Miriam her name, and when Fran repeats it—"Miriam"—her mother chimes in, "Miriam Batson. Did you ever know her daddy, Will Batson? Did you know him?"

All at once they're in Greenville again, as if Fran has a good chance of knowing Miriam's father, as so many people in Greenville once did. Fran leans closer, asks her mother to repeat what she has said. She's hard of hearing. Again her mother says the magic words: *Will Batson, did you ever know him?*

Her mother has forgotten where they are, she's forgotten that she's in Minneapolis, a town that means nothing to her. She's forgotten that she's old, decrepit, forgetful. She's somewhere else, back in Greenville, another time, another place. And Miriam is right there with her, floating outside of time and space, free, released. For this moment they've escaped the downward pull of her mother's old age, the weighty anchor of all they've lost. *Will Batson. Did you ever know him?*

Fran shakes her head. No, she doesn't think so. Miriam invites her to join them for coffee, but Fran is going back to her apartment to watch the news. And it is time, too, for Miriam and her mother to go. Miriam helps her mother back into the wheelchair and her mother, who has forgotten so much, remembers to ask Miriam where her pocketbook is. Miriam is ready with the answer. "Right here, Mother," she says, pointing to the chair where she had put it. "Right where we left it."

Not Ready

Miriam is not ready for the nursing home. Of course she's only (only!) forty-nine, and actually it's her mother who's the potential candidate, but nevertheless, Miriam is simply not ready. Not ready for the thin white towels that Penny, the nurse in charge, handed her tonight for her mother's room, after Miriam discovered her mother had no towels in the bathroom. Miriam was shocked: institutional towels. Each thing a small, accurate blow. Back home—"home" being her mother's apartment at the seniors' building, Wedgwood Manor, two blocks away—the towels are big, new, pink and blue. Miriam bought them for her mother about two weeks ago. Two new sets, one plush bath towel, one hand towel, and one washcloth in each set, the singleness of it all a kind of marvel to married Miriam, who had grown accustomed, without thinking of it, to buying towels in pairs. Her mother had complained of the mustard-colored towels that Linda, Miriam's sister, sent with their mother's things when they moved her from South Carolina to be near Miriam in Minnesota, five months ago. How had her mother come by those awful yellow towels in the first place? They were not, and never would be, Miriam's mother.

Nor, Miriam hoped, would these thin, generic towels she was draping over the metal bar of her mother's new room in the nursing home ever be. The room smelled— there was no getting around it—like urine. Not pee, which implied something non-offensive and transient, but urine—entrenched, institutional, forever. Since the smell would never come out, that meant Miriam had to get her mother out. She had spent all afternoon getting her in, and now, in a cartoon-like reversal, she saw herself spending all the next day getting her out. Miriam just was not ready for the nursing home.

She wasn't sure if her mother was ready or not. Her mother had been so compliant about the whole thing. She seemed to trust Miriam, who was feeling incredibly harried and worried about making the right decisions. They had spent all day, from ten in the morning until five in the evening, at the emergency room, in what Miriam was gradually coming to understand was not an emergency. Her mother had fallen again that morning, and now she was in a nursing home. Hopefully just for a night or two. At least that was what Miriam had in mind. It was mainly so that Miriam wouldn't have to spend the night with her; she was worn out from spending the day with her. And she couldn't tell whether her mother could walk well enough to be left by herself. She couldn't, really, but that was nothing new. That was why she had fallen again. But where did that leave them? Either putting her in a nursing home permanently, where she could be semi-protected by sitting in a wheelchair all day, or continuing to take the risk of letting her live in her own apartment. She might not fall at all (unlikely), or she might not fall for six months (hard to say), or she could fall tomorrow and break the proverbial hip. But wasn't taking that chance better than the urine-smelling nursing home?

Miriam thought of putting her mother in a small box.

That would be the best way to keep her perfectly safe. A little silver box, like the one on her mother's dressing table in the apartment. It was hard to keep anything safe, really. Especially a person. Double especially an old person. You had to suffer risks. That was how Miriam thought of it, at least. It made her suffer to take the risk of having her mother live on her own, in her own apartment. It made her suffer to think of the time that would probably come, sometime, when her mother actually broke something. The hip seemed the true watermark. If her mother ever actually broke her hip, Miriam figured that she herself would fall down wailing. Breaking a hip was The End. At least that's what Miriam heard when all the "professionals" said, *We wouldn't want her falling down and breaking a hip*. As if Miriam would, did.

But she couldn't keep her mother in a little silver box. Oh, those damn rings! Miriam's mother kept her rings in that little silver box on her dresser. She was sure someone was going to steal them. A diamond ring. A ruby. Her wedding band had a gray piece of string knotted around it a few dozen times, to make it stay on. Her mother's fingers, like the rest of her, had shrunk. They looked somehow elegant and also creepy to Miriam, old-lady hands, the fingers kind of strangely crooked and really long, the nails in need of a manicure. They looked exactly as Miriam remembered her grandmother's hands looking, gnarled, bony, a raised relief map of blue river veins and brown desert splotches. Old hands.

Why did this particular association, that her mother's hands had turned into her grandmother's hands, make Miriam so uneasy? If her mother had turned into her own mother in old age, then Miriam was becoming *her* mother in middle age. But she still thought of herself as young! Wasn't she still the granddaughter, the perpetual granddaughter, and not the worn, responsible woman who used to be her mother caring for her own mother?

What a dirty trick! In aging, her mother had dragged Miriam along with her, forcing her to wade into the river of time, to be swept along with the rest of them, everybody, humanity. Miriam had wanted to stay on the bank, dry, playing as it were, ignoring the fact that she herself was aging. Okay, *dying*. But here came her mother to point it out to her by turning into Miriam's grandmother, nursing-home material. For when the time came, Miriam's mother had put her own mother into a nursing home.

How had they gotten into this situation, Miriam checking her mother into a nursing home? Not a permanent placement, just an overnight or two or three, until her mother could return, hopefully to her own place. It cost the same as a good hotel room to spend the night at the nursing home, and Miriam hoped her mother would see it that benignly. "Mother," she had tried to explain at the emergency room, "you're going to spend the night somewhere where there'll be people to look after you, until we can see how you're doing." She was careful not to mention the term "nursing home."

"Do whatever you think best," her mother had said wearily. "I'll leave it up to you."

But Miriam didn't want the decision left up to her, even though she had already made it. She was so accustomed to so many years of her mother being perfectly cognizant, totally in control, really, that it was still hard for her to adjust to the notion that her mother didn't track everything the way she used to. She wasn't sure, any more, how much her mother really understood. Dementia, the doctors called it, though Miriam's mother was hardly out of her mind. It was more as if her brain had shrunk, like the rest of her. Miriam could feel her mother leaning on her, mentally as well as physically, letting Miriam make the decisions. Miriam expected to be bowled over by this weight, the weight of her mother leaning on her and letting her take over. She still felt like that frail girl, the granddaughter, not a grown-up (supposedly). But at least she bore up. She bucked up. She did the best she could.

Like this morning, when Miriam had called her mother to check on her, as she did every morning. She had let the phone ring maybe twenty times; it often took her mother a good while to get to it.

"I fell and hit my head," her mother announced a bit breathlessly.

"What!" Miriam couldn't help shrieking, though she did manage to contain the alarm somewhat. "What happened, Mother? Where did you fall?"

"I'm not exactly sure …" her mother trailed off.

"Are you sure you fell?"

"Well, I think so. The back of my head is sore as a boil when I touch it. And this … this …" Her mother had trouble finding the right word sometimes. "Something is knocked over," her mother finished lamely.

Miriam got in her car and zoomed over to Wedgwood Manor. As she came down the hall towards her mother's apartment door, she saw that the newspaper and her "I'm okay" sign had been taken in. It couldn't be too bad a fall, Miriam figured, otherwise her mother couldn't have gotten to the door with her walker and unlocked it to take in the sign and paper.

And indeed, she found her mother in her bathrobe, sitting in the big pink chair in her bedroom, her champagne-colored hair (it surely was snow-white under the dye) a bit disheveled, a knot forming on the back of her diminutive skull, but otherwise much as always. Conscious, communicating, but not able to remember what had happened—

nothing new there. Her mother had lost the ability to remember recent events, from whether she had eaten her
last meal to the answer to a question she had just asked.
She retained her general intelligence, but her memory had
lost its sticky surface.

The ominous thing, however, was that the closet door,
a sliding mirror, had been knocked off its runners. Her
mother had fallen against this mirror door with enough
force to dislodge it. She could have hit her head against it,
jarring her neck or spine. Maybe she had landed hard on
her hip. Miriam got her up, and her mother moved slowly with her walker towards the bathroom. So she could
walk, which seemed to Miriam a great sign, a sign that
nothing, in fact, was broken.

As they inched their way to the bathroom, Cathy arrived. Cathy was her mother's latest home health aide,
there to give her her Wednesday morning bath. After an
initial discussion about the fall, which by now her mother
couldn't even remember had happened, Cathy and Miriam got her onto the stool in the bathtub. They didn't dare
lower her all the way into the tub, for fear they'd not be
able to get her back up. But her mother sat on the stool
and enjoyed the bath.

Miriam had never met Cathy before, and she watched,
fascinated, as Cathy tended her mother. She called her
"chum" a lot. It struck Miriam as amazing that her mother had ended up being called "chum" by a kindly, middle-
aged dyke, as Cathy seemed to be. But her mother clearly
liked Cathy, and praised her for being efficient, professional. Cathy, her thin white blouse wet from the bath
and revealing huge, pendulous breasts, sweating below
the hairline of her close-cropped, graying hair, was cheery,
strong, and willing to cut her mother's gnarled yellow toe-
nails, something Miriam herself was loathe to do.

It was Cathy who insisted that Miriam call her mother's doctor's office to see "what to do" about the fall. Miriam herself was debating ice or heat, and she really saw no reason to call the doctor. At this point she still had her wits about her, remembering the cardinal rule: *Never involve medical personnel unless you absolutely have to.* But Cathy apparently had more faith in doctors than Miriam did, so finally, Miriam, under pressure, caving in to conscientiousness, called her mother's gerontologist's office. And got the predictable response from his nurse: She couldn't assess the situation over the phone, but what they recommended in the case of a fall was to take the fallee to the emergency room to be checked out and x-rayed if necessary.

Ah, that was a crucial juncture! Miriam could have stopped right there. Could have taken charge, trusted her own instincts that nothing was wrong with her mother that needed medical attention, and not given herself over to the system, such as it was. But Miriam was a chicken. She was afraid of doing the wrong thing; she felt so responsible for her mother, solely responsible, and that pressured her into always doing the conservative, overreactive, better-safe-than-sorry thing. Like taking her mother to the emergency room, even as some part of her knew—was screaming—that it was totally unnecessary, and would result, in fact, in exactly what it did result in: hours of wasted time, thousands of dollars in Medicare costs, and no help, no change, nothing, nothing, nothing.

But Miriam did have some experience with falls where her mother was concerned. She didn't think of it at the time, but later, musing over what had possessed her to take her mother to the emergency room that day—and then check her into a nursing home that night—Miriam remembered the Bad Fall and let herself off the hook a bit.

• • •

The Bad Fall had happened five years ago, coming a year and a half after Miriam's father's death, when her mother was making the hard adjustment (but did one ever make such an adjustment?) to being alone. She aged a lot in that first year of widowhood. Now when she needed someone to take care of her, Miriam was in Minnesota and Linda in Virginia. There were a few friends, aging themselves, and household help, mainly Frances three days a week, but her mother was becoming an old woman, bent and frail. And one day she fell. That was the way these things went, Miriam came to see. It was the body, finally, in its own eloquent way, that finally asked for help.

It had happened in December, when Miriam was on Christmas break from teaching. Aunt Ruth, not a real relative but a lifelong friend of her mother's, telephoned to say that Miriam needed to come. Miriam took a flight home to South Carolina the next day, arriving by taxi from the airport to find her mother curled in bed like a fetus. Aunt Ruth had been nursing her until Miriam could arrive. At first Miriam thought her mother was dying, she looked so small and shrunken. Miriam had trouble grasping the situation, never having had such an experience before. Her mother was so sore and stiff she couldn't get up, couldn't sit up, couldn't get to the bathroom on her own, couldn't do anything by or for herself.

The next day Miriam arranged for an ambulance to take her mother to the emergency room for x-rays. That had been the start of her maxim of never involving medical personnel unless you absolutely have to. It had almost killed her mother to be transported on the gurney down the stairs, to bump over the roads to the hospital, to spend time waiting and then lie on the hard board of the x-ray table, having to turn or be turned. Torture. And Miriam had made the decision to put her through it. So it was double torture, her mother's and Miriam's.

And of course, nothing helpful came of it. Her mother had a pelvis fracture, but there was no treatment, no help. That was Miriam's main feeling about that particular experience, and about many of the subsequent experiences involving her mother's old age: no help. You look around you and no one else is there. It's just you.

Miriam looked around her for help a number of times during the next three weeks. She took her mother home from the hospital, and then she became a nurse, round the clock. She slept, barely, lightly, in the bedroom across the hall from her mother. During the night her mother would call out Miriam's name when she needed to get up to go to the bathroom. Miriam would hear that absolutely familiar voice intoning that absolutely familiar sound: "*Miriam.*" She didn't know anything like it, it was so primal. The only other thing she could imagine coming close would be just the reverse, her own voice when she was a child, calling "Mama" in the night. At her name, Miriam would rise, as if from the dead. There was a definite feeling of resurrection about it, she'd be so tired, so exhausted from caretaking and anxiety and decisions. But as soon as her mother intoned that sound, Miriam was up and into the hall as if she had risen from the dead but lived again, was, in fact, extra-alive, electrified, even. She helped her mother, as her mother moaned from pain, try to swing her dead-weight legs around to the side of the bed, then half-lifted her onto her leaden feet. Together they'd shuffle to the bathroom. Sitting on the toilet was another form of hell for her mother, every movement a stabbing pain, a dog bite inside her skin. Then the laborious effort to stand back up, lumber back to bed, the lowering, swinging, easing back. At last, the lying down.

During the days there was so much to see to, to do. Miriam was busy every minute with tending to her mother, and time was passing, Christmas was approaching. It seemed she had been lolling, dreaming, for the first two weeks she was there, imagining that her mother would get better, back to normal, before Miriam had to leave. Then all of a sudden she got it: She had to make arrangements! She plunged into the whole world of social services, learning that in order to qualify for Medicare-paid nursing home care, her mother had to be admitted to the hospital for three days. They couldn't possibly pay for private nursing care at home, and they couldn't possibly pay for private care in the nursing home.

There were even problems with getting into a nursing home. Her mother's own mother had been at Oakview; there was at least a two-week wait there. It was a time of nerve-wracking crisis in which everything felt out of control, as if Miriam had been playing on the beach and suddenly got bowled over by a tidal wave.

Christmas Day was fast approaching, and Miriam was in a daze, a state of shock. Looking back now, observing herself from a distant future, she sees how lost she was, how frazzled. Evidence of this came on Christmas Day. She cooked a turkey. She cooked a whole Christmas dinner, in fact, as if by pretending to normalcy, she could manufacture it. Her mother couldn't possibly sit at the table, but Miriam got out a bridge table—oh, relic of her mother's former life!—and put it up in the bedroom, set a pretty table, and maneuvered her mother, through her pain, into the big pink armchair, stuffing pillows behind her. Her mother tried to sit up and eat the turkey, dressing, yams, and asparagus casserole—the food of Christmases past—that Miriam had hysterically prepared. But her mother could eat almost nothing and soon the party was over, her mother was back in bed, and Miriam was left with a lot of food and an incredible mess in the kitchen to clean up. She looked around her, but no one else was there.

Then her mother got constipated, seriously stopped up from the pain and medication and lying in bed, and somehow Miriam arrived at the moment when she herself and no one else had to give her mother an enema. It was called Fleet, a name Miriam turned over and over in her mind, conjuring up the curious associations of speed or naval ships. How did it get that name? A family name? Who would want enemas to bear their name? Not Miriam. She slunk around like a criminal at the drugstore when she bought it. It seemed childishly shameful, a dark secret, "excrement problems," something so private and distasteful that Miriam wished to be far, far away. But she was the only one around. Life had brought her to this moment, which involved squirting a vial of liquid into her mother's rectum as her mother lay curled on her left side in bed. Miriam stood there beside the bed, and at the last desperate moment looked around, willing someone else to be there to do this, to take over, to excuse her. It was one of those bald moments in life, when you realize that no one else is going to do it, whatever "it" is. You have to do it yourself. And she did.

Enemas seemed like the dark ages, a more primitive time. Her childhood, to be precise. Her mother had given her enemas when she was a child. It gave her the most uncomfortable feeling to remember this fact. She preferred not to think of it, she went for decades forgetting it, but it was true, it had happened, she had endured it, and probably the enemas had helped. She must have needed them. Her mother wasn't a sadist, after all. Miriam's grandmother, an old-country sort, had probably used the same remedy for Miriam's mother. And as she recalled (but why trust *her* memory?), it hadn't been a common occurrence, but a rarity. Maybe she should ask Linda. She pictures her sister's face when Miriam brings it up, long-suffering but patient, willing to help, probably wondering why Miriam doesn't remember herself.

But Miriam can't remember. She is the little sister, and she often turns to her older sister for information from that ancient time, their childhood. Sometimes Miriam wonders about the quality of her memory, which seems so poor. She's read memoirs by precocious writers who were precocious kids who took in everything, never forgot a detail, and can write it all down (it seems) as if they haven't forgotten a thing. But Miriam feels she lived through her own childhood in a sort of nonverbal, animal way. When she thinks of the enemas, vague and unpleasant images of some rubber tubing, orange, and an apparatus like a hot-water bottle come back to her. Something about water, feeling full, having to go. Was the bathtub involved somehow? How? It makes her squirm. The power her mother had over her, to do that thing, that intimate, unnatural thing, no matter how medicinal. It was at that moment when her mother was most The Mother, in charge, all-powerful, and Miriam was just a little animal-thing, helpless and at her mercy. Enemas were the start, perhaps, of wanting to get away from her.

Ah, the getting away and the coming back. Circle upon circle. Miriam's only, or at least best, defense against her mother's power was always to leave, to remove herself emotionally, then physically. She wasn't a real leaver, though; she always came back. Just as she was back, here, now, tending to her mother. An inexhaustible but exhausting continuum of duty and love.

How amazing it was to come full circle, to stand over her mother and help her in that particular way, flooding her bowels with liquid so that she could relieve herself. Maybe this was what family finally came down to, Miriam couldn't help thinking. You deal with the other person's shit, literally and figuratively. There was something so intimate in it, but also something impersonal in the end, something about flesh finally being just flesh. Looking down at her mother's big white bottom, Miriam felt a kind of wrenching compassion, not exactly for her mother, but for flesh, this mortal flesh.

So that was the Bad Fall. Finally it was decided that Linda would take time off from her civil service job when Miriam had to leave. She would come stay with their mother until their mother could be admitted to the hospital and then to the nursing home, for what they hoped would be short-term care, rehabilitation, and a return to her own home. They didn't know for sure that their mother would ever walk again.

When Miriam left she was wracked and grieving—prematurely, as it turned out—certain that this was it, The End, her mother having to go into a nursing home. Starting with that first Bad Fall, Miriam entered into a prolonged state of grief, one that continued to this day. That was what her mother's old age came down to, for her. But two months and a lot of physical therapy later, her mother returned to her own home. She lived on her own for five more years before Miriam and Linda finally moved her to Minnesota, to the apartment at Wedgwood Manor.

And now here she was again, five months into her new life, back in a nursing home. Whether for one night, or forever, Miriam couldn't say. She thought it was just temporary, until they could see whether her mother could walk the next day. They hadn't been able to tell Miriam anything helpful at the emergency room. After the initial wait to get processed for insurance, they had settled down for the long wait, the mother of all waits, in a small stall with a circular curtain that provided them with some visual, if not auditory privacy. Her mother lay on a hospital table; Miriam sat in a hard plastic chair. Together they listened to a loud-mouthed woman in the examining space on the other side of the curtain. Miriam and her mother had never been loud in their lives, and this woman was not only loud but profane, "common," as her mother would say. Miriam and her mother looked at each other. Her mother raised one thin eyebrow. "We have been so lucky in so many ways," she said to Miriam. Miriam nodded her head. She knew exactly what her mother meant. At that moment, she was filled with happiness: to be with her mother, to be together, the two of them still.

The afternoon dragged on, hour upon hour. Miriam began to get anxious. After some tests it became clear they weren't going to admit her mother to the hospital. That meant she would have to go back to Wedgwood, and that meant that Miriam would have to spend the night, unless she could find a home health aide, something her mother wouldn't like. She'd want Miriam, naturally. Miriam couldn't stand the thought of spending the night with her mother. What if it turned into another day and then another night, and on and on? She did have a life aside from her mother, a husband, a teaching job, though sometimes she wondered. What if her mother was practically paralyzed the next day, the way she was after the Bad Fall? Miriam couldn't face it. *I can't take this on*, she wanted to say, *I'm not up to it, I'm too young, too frail, just a granddaughter really.*

She had the hospital social worker try to find a home health aide, but it was too late in the day to line anyone up. The social worker suggested a nursing home associated with Wedgwood, a kind of temporary arrangement until they could see how her mother would do. In the abstract, it had seemed a good idea. Miriam liked the idea of unloading her mother, letting someone else be responsible for a while. It was almost five o'clock, the pressure was on, and she couldn't think very clearly, the day had veered so off track. She decided on the nursing home.

Deciding in the abstract at the emergency room was different, however, from wheeling her mother into the actual nursing home, at six o'clock that night, just in time for dinner with a lot of wrecked-looking souls. Miriam's mind told her this was a reasonable thing to do, but her heart screamed bloody murder. Her mother seemed beyond opinion for once, maybe dazed or exhausted. Miriam left her in the hands of Penny the nurse and rushed over to her mother's apartment to get her things for the night.

There was a profound absence when Miriam opened the door and stepped into her mother's apartment. She hadn't realized that absence could feel so palpable, the mirror image of presence. She was so used to her mother being there, her complaints, vulnerabilities, physical problems, and endless questions animating the air; she was not prepared for this emptiness. She got out her mother's overnight case, and put in a pair of pajamas and a bathrobe, looking around her for what else to take. Her mother would want her little pillow, the one she had had since she was a child, and her Metamucil and Correctol. Bedroom shoes. Toothbrush and toothpaste. A box of chocolates to ease the pain.

Something else was nagging at her, calling to her in its own silent language, but Miriam didn't know what it was. What? What else? Then she saw the little silver box on the dresser. She went to it and put her mother's rings in the change part of her billfold. She did this as if her mother were standing there, telling her to do so.

When she returned to the nursing home, her mother was back in "her" room, sitting in the wheelchair, and she seemed content enough. At least she wasn't upset.

"How was dinner?" Miriam said awkwardly, though her mother didn't seem to notice.

"I had to eat with all these … old people," her mother said. Miriam braced herself for her mother's ire, but it didn't come. Miriam felt surprised. The mother she knew would not put up with such a thing.

"I brought you some things for the night," Miriam said, and showed her mother what she had gathered.

"Did you get my rings?"

"They're in my purse," Miriam said. "I'll take them home with me."

Just then an aide, a young black man who might have been an African prince, knocked lightly on the door and stepped into the room. "Do you need anything, Mar-ie?" he asked her mother in a beautiful lilting accent. Miriam prayed her mother wouldn't use the word "colored."

"Not yet," her mother said, keeping her options open. Later he'll be wiping her butt, Miriam couldn't help thinking. Her Southern, practically Victorian mother had arrived at a point where an African man would be tending to her most intimate needs. Well, life took a number of unexpected turns, especially for the old.

She helped her mother into her pajamas and into bed. She raised the side rail. Her mother welcomed everything as it came, going along without resistance, complaint, or opinion. She wants to be taken care of, Miriam observed. Maybe it was too much of a struggle for her mother to live on her own, to take care of herself, with only Miriam to help. Was it only Miriam's idea that her mother should stay out of a nursing home, maintain (in a manner of speaking) an apartment? She had taken it for granted that her mother wanted to be independent, but now she wasn't sure. Miriam felt thrown off by her mother's acquiescence. Maybe her mother *was* ready for a nursing home, after all.

Miriam took the elevator down to the ground floor. On the way out, she passed an aviary where tropical birds flitted in the unnatural light. She paused to look at them. Some were nesting in little baskets hung from a wire frame stuffed with straw. A gray dove with orange rings around its eyes perched on a bare tree limb. A yellow canary stood in the middle of a dish of seeds. How contained they were, how safe. She moved towards the door and an electric eye spotted her, the glass doors opening automatically. It was dark out. Miriam went out into the cool summer evening, feeling strangely empty and greatly relieved to be free, as if she were one of those birds set loose from its cage, but lost in the wide world.

She awoke to a phone call after a toss-and-turn night. At first, she thought it was the middle of the night. But it was seven-thirty in the morning. Phone calls meant emergencies, and Miriam leaped from the bed. It was a nurse from the nursing home. "Your mother wants to speak to you," she said.

There was a long pause and some clattering of the phone as the nurse handed it over. The nurse must have brought her mother to the nurses' station in a wheelchair. Then her mother's voice broke through loud and clear. "Why haven't you come to get me!" her mother demanded. "I want out of here!"

Oh. So. Maybe her mother wasn't ready for the nursing

home after all.

The nurse got back on the phone and told Miriam she didn't see any reason why her mother couldn't return home. Miriam would need a doctor's authorization to get her out—the very thing she had needed yesterday to get her in—and the social worker would have to do the out-take papers. Since her mother had come in so late yesterday evening, they still had the intake papers to do, so this afternoon they'd do the intake and outtake papers at the same time. Miriam just groaned.

Over she went to the nursing home. "This place smells like urine," her mother complained. Her mother had survived the fall without any complications, it seemed. She could walk no better, but certainly no worse than she had before. It would be back to Wedgwood Manor.

Waiting and more waiting: for the doctor to call with the authorization to release her, for the social worker to come by with the intake and outtake papers. In the meantime, Miriam carried her mother's suitcase to the car.

It was after lunch before the social worker, a young, dewy thing, arrived. She called Miriam discreetly into the hallway. "Your mother has severe memory problems," she said breathlessly to Miriam, as if delivering breaking news. "She doesn't know what season it is!"

Miriam looked at her. She was maybe twenty-four, twenty-five. So this is what youth looks like, Miriam thought. This is a granddaughter, not me.

"That's okay," she said to the social worker. "Because I do."

Then she wheeled her mother onto the elevator and down to the first floor, past the aviary where the birds chirped away their little lives, and out the door into what was, plain to see, a fine summer day.

Home

Miriam moved her mother from South Carolina to Minneapolis when her mother became too forgetful and unsteady on her feet to live alone any longer. At first she lived in a senior citizens' building called Wedgwood Manor, in a one-bedroom apartment with a balcony. That lasted six months.

The depth of her mother's inability to live on her own was shocking to Miriam, who had fantasized some delightful times together in Minneapolis, as if her mother were a sturdy but intact oldster, and not the decrepit, dizzy, complaining, demanding, damaged person she actually was. To say she was forgetful was to mince words. Not that her mother wasn't still *compos mentis* in many ways. She struggled so to retain control of her life, and she was still sharp in certain ways, still so much herself, that Miriam had trouble grasping her deficits. Yet she was also amazingly, aggravatingly unable to manage the smallest things.

For example, her mother often called Miriam (she was still able to do this) to complain that she was burning up. It was summer, so naturally the apartment was hot. That's why it had an air conditioner. Miriam ground her teeth.

But that wasn't the real problem. The real problem was that her mother couldn't remember there *was* an air conditioner, let alone learn how to turn it on, and there was no one in the building to do it for her.

Little problems such as these, which came up every single day, were part of a bigger problem: Her mother needed to be taken care of. This was both her condition and her personality now, and Miriam couldn't separate the two. She'd get exasperated, she'd get sad, she felt sorry for her mother, she hated the way she was, a big hairball of mixed emotions.

But there were still good times. Case in point: Miriam and her husband, Ted, brought her over to their house to grill hamburgers on a Sunday afternoon that first summer, and she enjoyed the outing. Mother happy; Miriam happy. Mother unhappy; Miriam unhappy. Miriam was strapped to the wheel of her mother's emotions these days. That Sunday, sitting on their new, wrought-iron garden furniture, her mother laughed at a little joke that Ted made. Miriam stared at her mother laughing, wanting to remember that good moment: how beautiful the summer evening was, the grilled hamburgers like the ones they used to have at the cabin, baked beans and potato salad from Byerly's, her mother eating it all so happily. Miriam wanted things to be that perfect, always.

But the next day, when Miriam went over to her apartment, her mother was in the usual brain-damaged funk. She had been waiting all day for Kate, the college student who cleaned her apartment, but Kate didn't clean on Mondays. She cleaned on Tuesdays. Plus the caretaker's wife, Rachel, had been in to say that she was going to start cleaning for her instead of Kate. Miriam's mother was outraged. She was being treated badly. "They're trying to run over me." She had a way of misinterpreting things, taking them personally, acting out a kind of pompous indignation when she didn't get her way. Miriam saw this as her way of trying to hang on to some control, some power, throwing her (lack of) weight around. Her mother had always (always being when Miriam was growing up) been a person who both wielded power (of a domestic sort) as if it were her birthright, but was also (out in the world) rather timid. Was that true? How to get it right? As soon as Miriam tried to pin down her mother's personality, she was flooded with contradictory feelings and ideas, conflicting notions, qualifications, hesitancy.

Now she ordered Miriam in a mean, officious way, "Call the office and straighten it out!"

Miriam got her back up. "Mother, don't order me around! I'm not your servant!"

Her mother had a big bruise on her forehead, above her eye. How did she get it? Miriam had no idea. She irritated Miriam no end and crushed her heart. What a mix of powerlessness and willfulness, of meekness and feistiness she was. She was definitely self-centered and selfish. Miriam had trouble now knowing how much of that was her personality, and how much was old age. Her mother had always had a temper, been controlling, given to childish moments, but she had also been understanding, funny, forgiving, reasonable, competent, capable, mature. Your usual complex human being.

"Why don't we just drop it for now?" Miriam appeased.

"Because I can't think!" her mother screeched back. Miriam was taken aback. For someone suffering from dementia, she was certainly lucid.

Miriam tried to help. "It's not that you can't think, exactly, it's that you can't *remember*."

"I'm sorry I missed the distinction!" her mother bit back. She hobbled over with her three-pronged cane to sit in her blue La-Z-Boy rocker, which Miriam had bought for her when she moved her here, to avoid shipping the ancient yellow-green one from home. Her mother's balcony door at Wedgwood had blue, vertical curtain strips that closed like sideways blinds, left by the former tenant. Although they were not her mother's style, Miriam had punted and kept them, rather than order new window coverings. The matching blue chair was part of her effort to make everything about her mother's new living situation attractive, a real home.

But things were not going well. Right now, for instance, her mother looked lost, pathetic, and petulant. So of course Miriam did the only thing she knew to do: She fed her. Half her mother's lunch from Meals on Wheels was in the fridge: meatloaf, potatoes, Brussels sprouts. Miriam microwaved a small plate and fixed sweet ice tea, and her mother came to the little dining room table and ate it all. She was hungry and didn't know it, or maybe didn't know what to do about it. Miriam gave her a dizzy pill, a Meclazine, feeling a little guilty because she knew it would make her mother sleepy. A part of Miriam wanted to sedate her mother, perhaps permanently. The truth, which Miriam was trying not to see, was that her mother needed someone all the time, or at least nearby.

Miriam and Ted spent the Fourth of July at Ted's parents' cabin, with the rest of his family. The weekend was an agony for Miriam, who had to leave her mother completely alone for three days. She recruited one of the other residents to look in on her, but her mother didn't take to this woman and gave Miriam a hard time when Miriam told her how Lillian would be stopping in. "Oh I don't want that boring woman around," she said haughtily (as if she were fascinating herself). Miriam spent the weekend worrying and calling occasionally.

It wrenched her heart when she and Ted stopped by Wedgwood when they got back to town to find her mother standing in the hall with her three-pronged cane, dressed in a blue and white striped, satiny Sunday dress. Only extreme loneliness could have driven her mother into the hall. Normally she was afraid to leave her apartment, afraid she couldn't remember how to get back. At that moment Miriam saw that they couldn't go on. *She* couldn't go on. She needed help, she couldn't "do" her mother so much on her own. She'd have to move her again, only six months after she had uprooted her from her own home in South Carolina.

Miriam began to make phone calls. She had heard of a nice seniors' apartment building that had assisted living, which she had assumed her mother didn't need, when she first moved her to Minneapolis. It cost a fortune: more than $2,500 a month, a figure that was truly, deeply shocking at first, but once Miriam was desperate, it seemed quite manageable, hardly a concern at all. Not that they were rich. *Au contraire.* Her mother had Social Security and cash from selling her house, which was what they would spend down to keep her in assisted living. The money would last maybe three years; after that, it would be medical assistance. At any rate, her mother had enough money to go into assisted living, and a few days after she got back from the cabin, Miriam found herself looking at a new assisted-living apartment for her mother.

The apartment was in a building called The Kensington, in a lovely, elegant old neighborhood, one of the best in Minneapolis. Most of the fifteen-story building consisted of senior apartments, for people who were still independent. But The Kensington had divined that, as their population aged, they would need more care, so management had remodeled the fifth and sixth floors into assisted living. It seemed the best of all possible worlds to needy Miriam. Her mother could still have a one-bedroom apartment, thereby keeping most of the furniture they had sent up from South Carolina. They had kept the last, best things: the mahogany bedroom suite, the marble-top table, two living room chairs, a handsome mahogany chest of drawers, various hand-painted plates, and her mother's beautiful clothes. The good china, silver, and crystal were already distributed to Miriam and Linda, and a world of other things was gone, let go, disappeared. Her mother would have aides on duty twenty-four hours a day, plus nurses available from nine to five during the day. Miriam would not have to take care of her mother all by herself. She felt like falling on her knees in gratitude. Surely this was the solution to the problem they had.

Of course, getting her mother to move again was no picnic. Despite a daily litany of how she couldn't live like she was living, needed more help, couldn't go on that way, her mother declared that she liked her apartment just fine, all the problems involved in living by herself conveniently forgotten when Miriam broached the idea of moving. She balked when Miriam suggested The Kensington, "where she would have more help."

"I don't think I'd like it there."

"Mother, why not!"

A pause. "The atmosphere."

"But you haven't even seen it!"

No, she wasn't going to move. That was it. She had spoken. Miriam reasoned, argued, cajoled, half-realizing that her mother wasn't capable of making the decision herself, but unable to let go of involving her anyway. She wanted her mother to make the decision, take the responsibility.

Miriam was accustomed, after all, to forty-plus years of her mother knowing her own mind; it was hard to adjust to the idea that maybe she didn't have all the answers. Besides, this was her mother's life, and Miriam couldn't see just railroading her. Plus she didn't know how to. How do you move a person who doesn't want to go? *Someone please advise!* Nevertheless, Miriam was determined. She was a train moving relentlessly down a track. She was going to move her mother to The Kensington, come hell or high water. She had learned that phrase, not to mention the accompanying determination, from her mother.

Miriam wanted to show her mother The Kensington before she signed the lease. Miriam bargained. *Go over and see the place, have lunch there, and then decide.* But Miriam herself had already decided.

On the morning they were to go see The Kensington, her mother called Miriam at 7:00 a.m. to say she had had diarrhea all night and couldn't go. Miriam felt like killing herself, or better yet, her mother. Of course she had to go over to Wedgwood Manor and see about her. All the more reason to move her to The Kensington. "I'm too dizzy to get out of bed." Christ. But Miriam got her up and fixed her a boiled egg, toast, and tea. Her mother could no longer remember the diarrhea. Maybe she hadn't had it, after all. She felt better after she had eaten, and thought maybe she could go see The Kensington. Miriam had already called The Kensington to cancel, but now she called back to say they could come. She had canceled Meals on Wheels, then called back to reinstate the delivery when it looked as if her mother would stay home. Now she called to cancel the meal again. Then her mother started in again about how she wasn't going. "I'm too weak. I don't think

I can get dressed up." So Miriam called Meals on Wheels again, then The Kensington back to say that she would come by herself, without her mother. "Joking" about how they were crazy people, coming, not coming, coming. Too close to the truth to be funny.

At The Kensington, her mother would have three meals a day in the dining room, which was almost across the hall from the available apartment. An aide would help her get dressed in the morning and undressed at bedtime. There was housekeeping: Miriam wouldn't have to go over and see if her mother's trash was smelly! Someone would look in on her throughout the day. Theoretically, Miriam would be able to "enjoy" her mother more, instead of constantly being anxious and having to see to every little thing.

Miriam plowed ahead with plans for the move. She tried to prepare her mother, telling her how she forgot things. Her mother: "Are you blaming me for that?"

But gradually, as the month passed and Miriam held firm about the move, her mother came to accept it. Miriam and Ted finally got her over to see The Kensington. That made Miriam feel better, but an hour later her mother couldn't remember having visited it at all.

One morning right before the move, her mother called up: "I've been thinking. What are we to do about these phones!" Alarm in her voice: a problem!

Miriam, reassuringly: "We'll take them with us. I've already arranged for your phone service to start on Friday, so you won't be without a phone."

"Well, that's good," her mother said with relief.

"Everything is progressing smoothly for the move," Miriam told her.

"That's because of your ... personality," her mother

said in a halting way; she often had trouble finding the right word now. Miriam was touched, flattered even. It always made her feel good when her mother praised her. She still needed her mother's approval. Her mother often complimented her, thanked her for all Miriam did for her. At times their arm wrestling actually turned into an embrace.

Her mother had a way of rising to the occasion. The day of the move Miriam was over at Wedgwood Manor early to help her mother dress in a handsome, three-piece seersucker suit with narrow white and blue stripes, with white hoop earrings and a chain to match. Her mother sat on one of her two formal, ice-blue, matching living-room chairs and watched the movers pack up the apartment, supervising. Miriam was determined not to take everything, nor could she. The new apartment lacked a dining room, so they were giving the dining room table to Kate, the college student who cleaned for her mother and of whom her mother was fond. But that left two needlepoint chairs and a small glass-fronted cabinet. What to do? Her mother wasn't about to give them away. Stuff. Stuff, stuff, and more stuff. Miriam felt downright pissed, and not for the first time. Why hadn't her parents dealt with all their stuff during their lifetimes, when they were able! Why had they left it all for Miriam and Linda to hassle with, store, dispose of? Parents gave a lot, but they also made you pay. Miriam ended up arranging for the movers to cart the two needlepoint chairs, a nice knickknack cabinet that her parents had had always, the glass cabinet, and several boxes of stuff to her sister-in-law's attic. She assured her mother that she would come back for everything they left in the apartment later, when she had time. But her real intentions were to get rid of the dross.

Her mother entered The Kensington like a queen in a chariot, even if the chariot was her wheelchair. She knew how to play the role: gracious, dignified, charming. But wasn't she these things, after all? Miriam didn't really know. She just registered that she was proud of her mother, the way she might be proud of a daughter. The real estate agent with whom Miriam had signed the lease was there to greet them, as was the manager and the nurse on the assisted-living floor to which her mother was moving. Her mother greeted each warmly, as if she actually knew what was going on (did she?), holding her own beautifully, seemingly sharp. Miriam had arranged for them to arrive in time for lunch, so she took her mother to the assisted-living dining room across the hall and ate with her. Lunch was fine, except that one old lady at another table threw up her chocolate ice cream, an inauspicious beginning that almost made Miriam throw up, too, though her mother didn't seem to notice.

By four-thirty Miriam was exhausted and went home for a rest. But almost immediately she and Ted went back to have dinner with her mother in the main, independent-living dining room on the second floor. It seemed important to be with her mother on that first evening. The independent-living dining room had floral upholstered chairs, polite waiters and waitresses, big leather-bound menus listing the three entrees of the day, plus soup and salad selections, even lemon meringue pie for dessert. It was as if they'd moved Miriam's mother into a country club. Miriam ordered for her mother, who couldn't manage the menu visually or perceptually. The waiter brought soup and rolls. Miriam passed her mother a little pat of butter for her roll, but her mother put the butter in her soup.

• • •

When she and Ted left that night, an aide was already in her mother's bedroom, helping her get ready for bed. "Free at last," Miriam sang to herself. "Thank God almighty I'm free at last."

Not all that free, however. She called her mother first thing in the morning and got a big scare. "I fell," her mother exclaimed groggily, "and they've taken me someplace! To a hospital!"

What! Her mother had fallen and they hadn't even called her? The staff was supposed to call if a resident fell. And where was her mother? Miriam felt completely disoriented, as if she had dementia herself. Her mother must be in the "care suite" at the end of the hall, where they kept the worst-off residents who could afford to stay there, instead of going to a nursing home. At first, Miriam didn't register that she had called her mother's apartment and her mother had answered there. Her mother was quite incoherent, thinking she was in Greenville and Miriam in Minneapolis, and her confusion was catching. She said she had fallen two days ago, all mixed up. Through this strange conversation, Miriam gradually realized that her mother was in bed in her new apartment, and must have been dreaming that she'd fallen and been taken somewhere. It was both their worst fears, based on experience. Miriam felt shaken.

Gradually she oriented her mother, asking her to look around. Wasn't her big pink chair there in the bedroom, and what about her chest of drawers, and wasn't she in the four-poster mahogany bed she had slept in for sixty years? Ever so gradually, her mother came around and recognized her own things. But how awful it must be for her to wake up in yet another strange place, with only strangers to care for her.

• • •

On Saturday, Miriam went over to the Wedgwood apartment to finish cleaning out all that was left. Going into the apartment was hard on her. She had put so much effort into moving her mother there. She had wanted it to be so great. It really was a nice apartment—and now her mother was gone, like a little death. Miriam lay down, spread-eagled on the blue carpet, as if she needed her outstretched limbs to keep her from falling through the floor. She was free-falling through her own emotions. She thought about how she would run out and buy anything to make this apartment work for her mother, like the floor fan and the little TV for the bedroom, things she had no room for and that her mother couldn't use at the new place. What to do with the large flowerpots on the balcony? Miriam had planted them with geraniums and trailing petunias, so her mother could have a little garden out the sliding glass doors. But of course her mother couldn't go out there on her own. Even with Miriam, she was afraid of the height, because of her double vision and her messed-up depth perception.

Nothing was as Miriam had imagined. It had all been so intense, that was the thing. She'd been over here all the time, trying to tend her mother; her mother's presence pervaded the space. Miriam missed her. The sight of the last washcloth her mother had used, spread over the bathtub grab bar, tore her heart. If change was hard for her mother, it was hard for Miriam, too. She couldn't wait to get her mother moved out of this place. Now she mourned the life her mother had led here.

Miriam stood at the window where her mother used to stand to wave goodbye to her in the parking lot out back. She felt her mother's affection for her at those times, as well as her dependence, her need to wave goodbye, to see Miriam one last time, every time. It had been so painful to leave her mother alone, to know she ate every meal alone. Now she would eat with strangers every day. She thought of how her mother had called twice yesterday, when she and Ted were so busy moving the last of the stuff out of Wedgwood, leaving messages on the phone machine: "Could y'all come over and have lunch with me?" and later, "I'm back from lunch and y'all can come over now." Neither of which Miriam answered. She got so sick of her mother, her need, she could die or scream. But just thinking about it now, she picked up the phone that was one of the last things left in the apartment and called her mother at The Kensington.

A nurse answered the phone. Good. At least there was someone to look after her. She told Miriam her mother had high blood pressure and was dizzy. Normally her mother had low blood pressure, but the dizziness was nothing new. Miriam explained about her mother's habitual dizziness and recommended a Meclazine. The nurse said she might give the doctor a call, and Miriam left it up to her. She was practicing being off duty herself.

There were still some kitchen things to dispose of. They weren't moving any cooking items to The Kensington, because her mother wouldn't be cooking, ever again. Not that she had cooked at Wedgwood, but Miriam occasionally had. It had made her feel good that the possibility was there. Bringing some of these old, familiar pots and pans and whatnot from South Carolina to Minnesota had been less painful than getting rid of them when they sold the house. Now Miriam was stuck with them.

Miriam put a lot of kitchenware on the residents' give-away table in the first-floor laundry room. Almost as soon as she put things out, they were taken. She rode back to the apartment in the elevator, and the next time she rode down, swoosh, everything she had left was gone. Those seniors in the building really scarfed things up; word must be getting around. Like a secret elf, Miriam put out good items: the silk poinsettia her sister had sent to her mother last Christmas, pots and pans, dish towels and handmade aprons.

But of course there were still—still!—things Miriam either couldn't part with or didn't know how to get rid of. Like her sister's wedding picture. It was a big, full-length portrait of Linda in her fancy white wedding gown, framed in an ornate gilt frame. With its airbrushed, fairy-tale look of happily ever after, it had hung in their parents' dining room, even after Linda and Joe divorced. Her parents, unable to let go of the past themselves (so that's where Miriam got it), never took it down. The divorce had been painful for them. They hadn't known what to make of losing their son-in-law, so they just left the picture where it was, even though Linda had no interest in it, even though it probably brought her unhappy memories. Not knowing what to do with it either, Linda had shipped it to Minneapolis with their mother's things (on further reflection, their mother had probably made her). There was no room or reason to send it to The Kensington. But what was Miriam to do with Linda the bride? She carted her out to the car. She'd store her in the basement.

But how could she give away the old, clear-glass casserole they'd always used to put up the green beans her mother made with Miriam's father's white half-runners and a piece of fatback? They were the best beans in the world; their like would never come again. Holding that glass casserole was like holding a world, a lost world. She couldn't give it away. It was the cabin at Table Rock and summer mornings and her father striding in with tender green beans and her mother stewing those same beans over a hot stove, the four of them sitting down at the old pine table on the screen porch for corn bread, sweet stewed corn, the beans, fresh tomatoes, hot peppers, and cucumbers from her father's garden. Then one of "the girls" would put the leftover beans in this casserole. She'd never part with it. Someone would have to discard it when she herself died. Sorry.

The Kensington lasted exactly a year, and it was not a particularly smooth year.

A couple of days after the move, Miriam got a phone call about ten o'clock at night, long after her mother should have been in bed. Miriam had relished not having to talk to her mother that evening. To tell the truth, she was burned out. She had spent the better part of the day taking her mother to her doctor, and she was sick of the whole mess. As soon as the phone rang, she knew that it was her mother. She knew that ring.

"Guess what!" Alarm, fright, anxiety. "A big, black man came into my bedroom!"

Miriam was struck dumb for a moment. Then she understood. The man was an aide, of course, though she wished they wouldn't send men in to help frail old ladies into their pajamas.

"I'm sure he was an aide, Mother. Someone hired to help you. I wouldn't worry about it."

"Yes you would, Miriam," her mother said. "You know you would."

Not that assisted living wasn't an overall improvement. The nurses and most of the aides—a confusing mix of characters from week to week—were mostly kind and helpful. But they couldn't fill in for family. That much was clear. Her mother wouldn't go to the activities, and often she was dizzy, constipated, upset, or sad. So Miriam couldn't back off. She still had to "do" her mother in all sorts of ways. This was now Miriam's life, despite some lingering doubt that she should be living it this way.

On the periphery of consciousness, she sensed disapproval from certain friends, even from Linda. But not from Ted, who (despite his moments) had committed himself to supporting Miriam, knowing that it would be useless to try to change her anyway. She clung to this support, and to the idea, which he sometimes expressed, that Miriam knew what she was doing. She knew she wasn't doing it the "right" way. She knew, having breathed in the spores of the culture, that as a caretaker she wasn't supposed to let her mother's life take over her own. She was supposed to distance herself, turn her caretaking over to others. She was not unfamiliar with the term "manipulation." She'd mentioned to one of the nurses that her mother often complained to her, and the nurse replied that her mother never complained to the staff—keeping up a social front, Miriam knew instantly. The nurse said that old folks often complained only to their family members, and that this was a form of manipulation. An offhand remark. But Miriam had narrowed her eyes, taking it in. Did the nurse think Miriam was being manipulated? Did Miriam care? No.

Linda thought Miriam was being manipulated. "She's been manipulating you for fifty years." Their mother had sure known which daughter to end up with! More of her manipulation, no doubt. She had manipulated Miriam into taking her on, moving her to Minnesota. Boy, was she smart! But Miriam had a hard time seeing her mother as a manipulator, beyond the expected, accepted manipulation everyone is entitled to, of trying to get what they want.

What did Miriam's mother want? To be taken care of, to be a little happy, not to be alone, to feel secure, not to suffer, not to be neglected or mistreated. If she manipulated Miriam to try to get these things, more power to her. Miriam wanted these things for her mother, too. She couldn't bend her mind around the accusation of manipulation. She was dense, blocked in some way. Damaged to the core, no doubt, and by her own mother, the manipulator. She didn't even know enough to say no to her mother; truly, she didn't even feel her mother usually asked too much. That was because she didn't have to ask. Miriam was right there, anticipating her needs.

They struggled on, with good days and bad. There were more falls, and eventually a friend in the building, Kay, began eating dinner with her mother and even stopping by her apartment for an occasional visit. Kay, nearly blind from macular degeneration and practically deaf, had no family of her own to speak of. Sometimes they'd even hold hands, her mother reaching out her own bony, gnarled paw for Kay's bony, gnarled one.

But it was impossible to put together several good days in a row. There was always some mini-crisis, variations on the same theme. Miriam's mother wasn't doing well. At some point, a nurse suggested to Miriam that maybe her mother belonged in the care suite. Miriam was well aware of the closed door at the end of the hall. She regarded it with an irrational fear, as if it led to a gas chamber. In truth it opened into a suite of five rooms surrounding a common living area, and was the equivalent of a high-priced private nursing home. No! No! Miriam had exclaimed inside. Not the care suite! Didn't this nurse, this stranger who didn't really know her mother, understand that this was the end of the line? The End! No one ever came out of the care suite alive. It was the graveyard of assisted living. She was furious that anyone would suggest such a thing to her.

Still, at night Miriam was aware of a grinding in her sleep. She'd wake up with a tension headache. She always had a headache now. She had forgotten what it was like not to have one.

• • •

It was winter again, and the temperature was never right in her mother's apartment. She couldn't control the thermostat, didn't remember she had one, was dependent on someone to come in and adjust it. She was either "freezing" or "burning up."

"Miriam, I'm in the wrong place."

"Where do you think you should be, Mother?"

A pause. "Miami."

One night Miriam stopped by her mother's apartment to check on her, after having dinner with a friend. It was after eight o'clock, and her mother was in her pajamas, obviously engrossed in a TV movie, *The Joy Luck Club*. Miriam had read the book—all those conflicted mothers and daughters. They sat there together, her mother in the blue La-Z-Boy rocker, Miriam on the flowered sofa, watching a scene in which a banished daughter returns home as her mother lies dying. The daughter cuts her own flesh and stirs her blood into a soup to feed her mother. The words "pain," "sacrifice," "dutiful," and "daughter" flashed in subtitles across the screen. "Don't leave," the daughter begs her mother, the dying mother who had disowned her. "Don't leave, Mama." Miriam and her mother sat silently, breathlessly watching this scene, tears shining in their eyes.

II

Miriam began looking into nursing homes. She told herself she wanted to be prepared when the day came. Since she wasn't teaching winter term, she had time to investigate, get on waiting lists. But she was determined to keep her mother in assisted living as long as possible.

One night she dreamed she was riding an elevator, just like the elevator in her mother's building, but she couldn't get off on the correct floor for her mother's apartment. "I want to see my mother!" she kept insisting in the dream. "I want to see my mother!" But the elevator wouldn't stop on her mother's floor.

One day her mother called her. "I have a situation here I don't exactly know how to handle," she said. Miriam didn't even try to guess what it was. Sometimes her mother catastrophized. "The blind has fallen down! No one has made my bed!" Major upsets. But now she was saying something about someone hitting her.

The nurse was in with her mother when Miriam arrived. The woman across the hall, who had Alzheimer's and was getting more belligerent, had hit Miriam's mother on the head with a rolled-up newspaper at dinner, telling her she had no right, no right! They had already shipped that old lady off to the hospital (Miriam thought of the phone call *her* family would be getting), and she wouldn't be returning to The Kensington. Her mother seemed to take the attack in stride. "I thought this was a safe place," she said to the nurse. How could her mother process such a sophisticated thought? Miriam was often surprised by how much her mother got. At times she was definitely mentally competent. Surely the thing to do was keep her in her own "home" as long as possible.

Still, Miriam asked Ted to go visit the two finalist nursing homes with her. She was being realistic, after all, not trying to deny the inevitable. But really, she couldn't see moving her mother to a nursing home. Or rather, sometimes she could, and then she'd feel so bad, so sad, that she'd back off. Not until it was absolutely necessary.

In June her mother had a bad fall in the bathroom. "What about moving to the care suite?" Miriam broached, for gradually, over time, without Miriam knowing how or why, the care suite had come to seem highly desirable. Her mother wouldn't have to move to a real nursing home, she could stay in the building, she'd have more help there, the ratio of aides to residents was higher, there was more attention, more care.

Her mother looked alarmed, then angry, then obstinate. "Not down there where the babies stay!" she exclaimed. Miriam didn't know if her mother really thought they tended babies behind the closed doors, or if she was being sarcastic, referring to the failing, mostly mindless residents in the care suite as "babies."

"I will never go there," her mother proclaimed, and got upset and angry if Miriam brought it up.

Her mother was now taking Paxil for depression, and she was having crazy dreams. She'd wake up confused, disoriented. But then she'd come around, and they might go for a couple of days where things were more or less fine. Miriam took her to the nearby park in her wheelchair. They watched children wade in the cascading pools and talked about the past in snippets, reminiscing about other summer days when Miriam and Linda were children, and their mother took them to the beach every day at Table Rock Lake. On these park outings her mother would be calm, content, even happy. She loved seeing the children and the dogs that people brought. Miriam would decide they could, should go on in assisted living for as long as possible.

But then another fall, this time hurting her knee. She began taking her breakfasts in her room, having her tray brought in, not a good idea. Aside from costing extra, it seemed another indication that her mother wasn't able to manage even assisted living.

In July she fell out of bed, really hurting her leg. Her knee swelled, making it even harder for her to walk with her walker. Miriam rushed out guiltily and bought a bed rail. Why hadn't she thought of it before! She knew instinctively it must be the Paxil that had caused her mother to roll out of bed. She had the doctor take her off the medication, and the crazy dreams stopped.

What had seemed so necessary to Miriam a year ago, the big one-bedroom apartment, was now an endless territory for her mother to traverse. She had miles to go from the bedroom to the bathroom. Even the living room looked huge as her mother rose shakily from her blue La-Z-Boy and started toward the door to the hall with her rolling walker. She was still alone most of the time. The aides were overworked and the nurses couldn't spend all their time with Miriam's mother, as she would have liked.

It was the second summer her mother had lived in Minnesota, and Miriam and Ted scheduled a one-week vacation in Northern Wisconsin. Linda came to look after their mother while they were gone. When Miriam and Ted returned, she and Linda would take their mother on a little weekend vacation, in honor of all the vacations they used to take together. They had reserved a cabin on Lake Superior, with a ramp for her mother's wheelchair. The cabin had a deck and Miriam pictured the three of them, family, having cocktails (ginger ale for their mother these days), and cheese and crackers out on the deck before some wonderful summer dinner that Linda and Miriam would whip up. The very thought made Miriam deeply happy.

It took about three days on her own vacation with Ted, but finally Miriam really relaxed. Her sister was looking after their mother, and Miriam was off call. Even her headaches went away as she lay on Madeline Island's sandy beach, eyes shut against the bright summer sun.

They got back to town about four-thirty on Friday afternoon, and were planning to have dinner at The Kensington with Linda and their mother. Miriam noted that her headache returned as soon as she walked in the door of her own house. Still, she felt eager to see her sister and mother, eager to go on the little vacation "the girls" had planned. She rang her mother's apartment and Linda answered.

"She fell again this morning," Linda said. "She's hurt herself to the extent that the trip is out. You'll have to call and cancel."

Miriam's mother had fallen on her face. She looked like a raccoon, both eyes blackened where her glasses had bruised her. She had hurt her leg again. The time had come.

III

It took Linda and Ted to make the decision. Miriam could not do it on her own, even though she knew it was inevitable, for the best—even though she longed for it. The nurses at The Kensington helped out, saying, when they grasped what was needed, that they didn't really feel they could take care of Miriam's mother properly anymore. It was clear to everyone, even to Miriam, that her mother needed to be in a nursing home. But that didn't mean it was easy.

Miriam marveled at how thoroughly she had done the groundwork. She had visited a number of nursing homes over the winter, as if she *knew,* (*but I never believed!* Miriam exclaimed deep inside), and had narrowed the choices to two. How handy, how efficient! And wonder of wonders, Linda was there to help out. The moment was unavoidable, and yet … and yet … It was easier for Linda, Miriam sensed, who wasn't so invested in keeping their mother in assisted living. She could see the forest clearly, while Miriam was lost, as usual, in the trees: the endless visits to her mother at The Kensington, trying to keep her afloat, bailing a sinking ship. Miriam had bailed so diligently, so frantically, as if effort were any match for an aging, failing parent. It was good, Miriam saw, that Linda was there to make the decision really, help with the move, share the load. Miriam sensed, through a fog of pain, that Linda was taking charge, making the decision (though Miriam pretended she was doing so, too) for Miriam's sake—something Miriam was incapable, it seemed, of doing herself.

She and Linda visited the two finalist nursing homes first thing Monday morning. Social workers at nursing homes, it turned out, were accustomed to situations such as theirs—the last straw, the sudden emergency. The first finalist was an inner-city facility that had a good reputation and had been recommended by their mother's doctor. But it was no-frills, a basic, efficient, clean, institutional residence, which did not impress Linda. She indicated this by not saying much, which naturally Miriam could read, knowing her sister as she did. Around her big sister, Miriam had a great propensity to become the little sister, deferring to Linda's obviously better judgment. Miriam kind of liked the first one, mainly because it had the possibility of a private room. She fixated on that, unable to imagine moving their mother to a semi-private room.

On to the other finalist. It was as genteel and prettied up as the other had been plain and simple. "Now this is more like it," Linda said, as they toured the facility. Unlike the other nursing home, it had an assisted-living section and maintained the appearance of a gracious, senior apartment building, much like The Kensington. There were various lounges with formal, handsome furniture, a library and crafts' room, a small private dining room that could be reserved for special occasions, a reception desk surrounded by a large living area where the better-off old ones sat to read the newspaper or could visit with friends.

The nursing-home sections, on the second and third floors, were more institutional. Still, they appeared well run, and the nursing staff was friendly, even warm. Best of all, the place, called Jackson-Wilkens, was on a beautiful piece of property right in the city, right on Cedar Lake, surrounded by old-growth trees. There was even a distant view of the Minneapolis skyline. "Perfect," Linda proclaimed. "I can really see Mother here."

At least Miriam had picked it out as a finalist. She was still smarting a little from Linda's swift rejection of the first home. She had been told, on her previous visits (two! She had brought Ted the second time) that the waiting list for a private room at Jackson-Wilkens was about a year long. But lo and behold, there was not just one private room available now—there were two. Miracle of miracles. Linda and Miriam could not believe their luck. Their luck, of course, was someone's demise. Later, as Miriam came to see, turnover was neither a miracle nor even unusual.

One of the available rooms had a view of the lake! If only they could get that room! It might already be spoken for: suspense. The social worker would have to let them know. But Jackson-Wilkens was prepared to take their mother immediately; it could, in fact, only hold a room for her for a day or two. They'd have to move fast.

Things were going a little too fast for Miriam. She had expected to be on the North Shore with her mother and sister, eating cheese and crackers on a deck, and now she was about to move her mother to a nursing home. They were about to move their mother into one room. Actually, one room seemed an enormous luxury, compared to what most people had: a semi-private room sharing a bath. But still.

Miriam thought of her mother's Kensington apartment, which she knew so, so well. What would they do with all her mother's things, her beautiful things? They had winnowed eighty-plus years of material life down to what a one-bedroom apartment at The Kensington could accommodate. Now they had to reduce it all to one room? Miriam's head spun. And how were they to persuade her mother to move? She remembered what they had gone through in moving her mother from South Carolina to the Wedgwood to The Kensington. Miriam knew her mother wouldn't go without a fight. She was a survivor, and you didn't survive, Miriam was coming to understand, without some fight. Otherwise, life just mowed you down. Actually, it mowed you down anyway.

"The girls," as they had always been to their mother, were nervous. They might both be over fifty, well into middle age and more-or-less responsible citizens (the less being Miriam, who didn't seem capable of holding a nine-to-five job; the more being Linda, who held a big, super-responsible job for which she left the house at 7:00 a.m. and didn't return most evenings until after 6:00 p.m., provided she didn't have an evening meeting). But where their mother was concerned, they were still the girls.

Miriam remembered the time Linda, who was maybe fifteen or sixteen at the time, was carrying their dog Blaze's food in a boiler pot down the stairs in their split-level house on Paris Mountain in Greenville. She tripped and dumped all the wet kibbles mixed with canned dog food onto the rug at the bottom of the stairs. "Ma—ma!" Linda had shrieked. It was a complex moment. Miriam, at the top of the stairs, was wide-eyed in shock but also already laughing, out of a mixture of nerves (their mother would be furious), and the hilarity of her sister dumping dog food on the rug, the comic pratfall of it all. Her sister was scared of their mother's reaction but also needed to "'fess up," to call down their mother's wrath and also the possibility of salvation. It was kind of a biblical thing, when you came right down to it. Their mother as God, able to smite them down with a word or look, but also able to save them from eternal damnation. Miriam could no longer remember the outcome—Linda had to clean it up, no doubt—but that poignant wail lingered still in her mind: "Ma-ma!" Full of fear, longing, need, surrender.

Things were moving very fast. It was already Tuesday, Linda was leaving on Friday, and Jackson-Wilkens would only hold the room for a couple of days. Miriam and Linda needed a doctor's order and were waiting to hear if the room with the lake view was available. Meanwhile, they had to tell their mother that she was going to be moving yet again. Time to haul out "reason." Miriam's mother had always had a practical, realistic side, a down-to-earth, face-the-facts quality they could count on. Only now, they weren't sure exactly how much their mother really understood about her situation. It was hard to tell, because she was such a skillful compensator, appearing quite capable mentally in some ways. They knew she couldn't make such a decision for herself; no one should have to. But out of respect for her, and habit, they wanted to tell her what was going on, and why, as much as possible. At the same time, they didn't want to unduly upset her (or themselves).

They brought in The Kensington nurses to explain that they could no longer take care of her there. In the new place she'd have more help; their mother's perennial battle cry: *I need more help!* Their mother seemed to accept this reasoning. Miriam was beside herself with joy. She looked on her mother with love and admiration; boy, was she great. She really could pull up her socks when the going got tough. After all, she had put her own mother in a nursing home, so it wasn't exactly unknown to her that there came a time when a nursing home was not only inevitable, but the best thing. Not that they had actually used the term "nursing home," but still: a place with more help. Nursing homes weren't what they used to be, exactly, anyway. More enlightened, less warehousing. Weren't they? They had to be. Why hadn't Miriam recognized this before!

So. The girls had got past the hard place, or at least one of the hard places. They went home to Miriam's to make their plans. Now they had to decide about all the things their mother couldn't take from the apartment. Hardly any of her old, huge things were appropriate for the one room she'd have in the nursing home: certainly not the massive mahogany chest of drawers with the huge gilt-framed mirror above, not the beautiful, antique marble-top table that their mother had owned since she was first married. They had a photograph of her as a beautiful young woman standing next to the table, slender and full of the future, lit by the hand-painted glass globe lamp that still sat at The Kensington on that marble-top table fifty years later. What to do with these things?

Linda would take the marble-top table and antique lamp, and the living-room sofa that Miriam had specially ordered just a year and a half ago when she moved her mother to Minnesota. The chest of drawers would have to go. Miriam would take the bedroom suite her parents had slept in: the dark mahogany bed, with its beautiful headboard and four turned posts, the dressing table with its suspended mirror, two bedside tables, and a large matching chest of drawers. How her mother had loved that bedroom suite. At the nursing home she would sleep in a single bed with rails, keep her pajamas and underwear in a fake-wood chest the facility provided, use their utilitarian bedside table and vinyl chair with sturdy arms that would help her get up from it. The only concession to home was her La-Z-Boy rocker, a few pictures for the wall (air-brushed formal portraits of Linda and Miriam in high school, looking nothing like their real, flawed selves, and some needlepoint pictures their mother's aunt had stitched), and the giant TV.

Wednesday morning. Linda and Miriam were at home, waiting for the call that would tell them whether they could have the room with the lake view—a sort of salvation in their minds, as if that room justified everything—and also for word from the doctor, who would write an order for their mother to be admitted to a nursing home. Their mother was still ailing from her recent fall, so one of them would have to go to The Kensington while the other waited for the calls. Miriam felt she should stay home and Linda should go over to see about their mother. Miriam would come when she had received the calls and made whatever plans she could about moving the furniture from The Kensington.

But there was only one car. Miriam suggested Linda ride the bus to The Kensington; Miriam would drive over later. But Linda balked. She seemed to have never heard of riding a bus—apparently they didn't do that sort of thing in the part of Virginia where she lived. It's no big deal, Miriam persisted, it's a direct route, you don't even have to change, just get off a block from The Kensington. Suddenly they were at each other's throats, figuratively speaking. Their way of fighting was to withdraw in a cold fury, to sulk rather than speak. Miriam barely stopped herself from slamming a door as she fumed out of the room. She had never met anyone so unreasonable, so obstinate, so immature, so uncooperative as her sister! She couldn't stand her, really. She couldn't wait for the moment when she'd leave. They'd never gotten along, this seeming team effort of dealing with their mother a thin façade, they were totally different, she'd never want Linda for a friend, she couldn't abide her!

Miriam was miserable. She couldn't stand her sister, she had to put her mother in a nursing home, they might not get the room with a view. When Linda flew away she would be left not only to deal with their mother but also to empty The Kensington apartment. Miriam was prone to feeling overwhelmed, and if she could have she would have lain down on the bed with a cold, wet washcloth on her forehead. Only there was never time for such theatrics. She had to talk to her mother's doctor's nurse, then go through a few hundred rounds with Linda: "I'll take the bus, no you take the car, no you take the car and I'll take the bus, no, you, no you, no let me" until they were both worn out with contriteness, nerves, tension, and a kind of raw pain. They could never tolerate being mad at each other for long.

The call came from the nursing home: the room with the lake view was theirs. Hurrah! The answer to their prayers, such as their prayers were at this point. They went to The Kensington together in the car and asked their mother if she'd like to see the "new place" they had in mind for her. The place with "more help." Where there would be nurses around the clock and plenty of aides (*wouldn't there be?*) and a lovely room with a lake view. "They won't hold it for more than a day or two," Linda said in a phony, solic-

itous voice, as if she were talking to a balky child. Their
mother, probably pleased to have her two daughters there
and trying to cooperate, agreed to go have a look. This
was going better than Miriam could ever have imagined.
If their mother hadn't been present, she and Linda would
have high-fived each another, co-conspirators, maneuver-
ing together through the delicate shoals of moving their
mother to a nursing home.

They pushed their mother, with her raccoon face, in a
wheelchair through Jackson-Wilkens that afternoon: *Isn't
this nice, Mother! And this would be your room, see, with
the view of the lake! Isn't it beautiful! Boy, think what
this property is worth, right in the city and yet it feels like
you're in the woods. And see, there's downtown Minneapolis.* Their mother pretending to peer through the window, her double vision creating not one, but two skylines.
Well, what do you think? Whatever you girls think is best.

Miriam couldn't believe how smoothly things were going! Her mother was acting like such a grown-up, so mature. Which of course, at eighty-seven, she was. Sometimes
it was hard to remember that she had all this life experience to draw on, not to think that because she had dementia, she was a child. She wasn't. She was an old woman,
struggling to do the best she could with what she had left.
It was moving to behold.

That night, as Miriam, Ted, and Linda sat around having a stiff drink and congratulating themselves on their
success, they got a phone call from Miriam's mother at
The Kensington. "I've decided to stay here," she said. "I
want to stay with my things a while longer."

Miriam, who answered the phone, felt a familiar feeling. Just when she thought something involving her mother was going to work out, it did a complete flip. Now
her mother had spoken. She was not going to budge, at
least not without a struggle. Miriam pictured a cat being

forced into a box, its paws braced against each corner of the opening in stiff resistance. That would be her mother when they tried to force her out of her apartment at The Kensington. She'd brace against the doorframe with all fours, lock-jointed. She'd somehow surfaced from her memory loss to realize she'd be leaving her beloved things. That much she grasped. She was begging them not to do that to her, in the only way she knew how, which was to order them. "I've decided to stay here," she said, as if her life were still her own.

Linda and Miriam made their evil plans. Miriam felt like a character in *Macbeth*, conspiring to commit bloody murder. They'd go to The Kensington in the morning and take their mother out for lunch before taking her to Jackson-Wilkens for good. There would be a brief chance to say goodbye to the kind souls who had tended her at The Kensington. If they ran into trouble, if her mother acted up, they'd bring in the heavy artillery: the head nurse who would tell their mother that she could no longer stay there, because they couldn't take care of her any longer. True in a way, though it was not the nurse or The Kensington that had made the decision to place their mother in a nursing home. It was her girls. They wouldn't take a thing with them. They'd return for her pajamas and overnight things later that afternoon, after they had delivered her to the nursing home. Better to just leave. Out to lunch with the girls, and then … Miriam couldn't bear to think of it.

They were both nervous the next morning, wondering what the day would hold. They'd put out a nice dress for their mother, and an aide had helped dress her and fixed her face. Their mother seemed calm. She appeared to know what was going on, though nothing too direct was said. Linda and Miriam told her they'd go out to lunch, and then go to Jackson-Wilkens, *remember, the place we went to yesterday?* Their mother did not remember. Maybe their mother's memory loss was actually a blessing. As her body failed, her mind did, too, not letting her remember all the daily injustices, losses, and indignities.

One by one, the aides and nurses who had cared for their mother for a year came in to say goodbye. She had been a favorite, it seemed—though maybe they said that to everyone. Still, their mother did have charm. She could be so gay and friendly, so warm and appreciative. Miriam was proud of her all over again, as she often was, the doting mother herself. Their mother seemed to know that she was leaving. "Come see me," she said as she took kind hands. "You know where to find me." They all said they would. And then it was time to go. Miriam and Linda cut their eyes at each other over the top of their mother's wheelchair. *This is it.*

"Are you ready to go out for lunch, Mother?" Linda asked brightly. She held the knife behind her back.

"I better go to the bathroom first," their mother said. What else was new? Miriam wheeled her in to the bath, helped her stand and turn around, instructed her to "hold on while I pull down." She was so used to having her face near her mother's butt. The big, white doughy flesh, the mild stink of undies, the tinkle of her mother's pee. This would probably be Miriam's most enduring memory of her mother's old age: the intimacy of this toilet tableau.

Then it really was time to leave. Miriam felt slack-jawed with sorrow. *Look around you, Mother,* she wanted to say, but didn't, couldn't. *You will never see these things again—your things that are you, that you love. We are ripping you away from them, stripping you of almost all that you cherish, of the things that are left of your life. You are leaving through that door, and you don't even know it and we can't tell you, because it would be unbearable. And it has to be done. I'm saying goodbye for you, Mother. Goodbye to all this. Goodbye to what's left. I'm so sorry, Mother. I've done the best I could.*

They chose a lunch place near Jackson-Wilkens. Miriam had checked out the nearby handicapped-accessible restaurants that tolerated decrepit old folks. Toby's seemed to specialize in seniors. There were always plenty of customers coming early, leaning on walkers or pushed in wheelchairs by their aging children. The restaurant served gigantic popovers, which Miriam's mother loved. Miriam pulled the airy dough apart and spread butter on it for her, trying to give her something on this day she could enjoy. Their mother was in a good mood, even festive. This was a treat, having lunch out with her two beloved daughters. Linda helped her order spaghetti, something she could handle if they cut it up for her. But their mother was full by the time she finished the popover. "I can't eat all this!" she exclaimed, and tried to foist off the spaghetti on Linda and Miriam, who were struggling with their own heavy lunches and no appetites. Her desire to feed them was just as strong in her old age as it had been when she was a young mother, sticking spoonfuls of pureed carrots in their uncoordinated mouths, saying *Here comes the choo-choo train, open up the tunnel.*

Agony. Watching the clock. They were supposed to arrive at Jackson-Wilkens around one-thirty. That was when the social worker and charge nurse would be ready to do intake. Intake. They were about to enter an institutional world. They were through with their lunch, but it was only quarter till one. They tried to talk their mother into dessert. "I couldn't possibly. You girls have some." Linda and Miriam looked at each other miserably, grim-faced. Might as well go. Miriam felt she might float away, unmoored, as if she were filled with helium and could rise like a balloon and disappear into the pale blue sky.

Another bathroom trip, this time Linda's chance to stick her face close to their mother's butt. Did their mother have any idea what was transpiring? Miriam wondered, paying the bill absentmindedly. She seemed so happy, so gay, really. Miriam couldn't remember seeing her mother so joyful in recent years. It was striking. Maybe moving to a nursing home was what her mother actually wanted! Maybe it would put an end to her anxiety about who would take care of her. Their mother had always been smart. Maybe she knew it was the absolutely right, best thing! Amazing how things work out.

"This is going better than I ever could have dreamed!" Miriam exclaimed to Linda, after they had gotten their mother into the car and were hoisting the wheelchair into the trunk together.

"I know," Linda said. "She really seems to be accepting it. She seems relieved, like she's glad the decision is made."

"Amazing!" Miriam said.

To exit the restaurant parking lot, Miriam had to drive around the building, close to its sidewalk curb. They passed within a couple of feet of a fat man who was bending over to tie his shoe. His rear end in shorts appeared almost in their mother's car window. Suddenly Miriam's mother yelled, "I see a BIG BUTT!" Miriam couldn't believe her ears. She and Linda burst out laughing, astonished. Their mother was laughing, too. "Well, it was practically in my face," she said.

They were all laughing hysterically (with the emphasis on hysterical, Miriam would note later), tears running down Miriam and Linda's faces. Miriam had the strange sensation, an almost out-of-body feeling, that they were three girlfriends out on a lark. They might as well have been in a convertible with the top down, yelling out naughty and flirtatious things to boys they passed, the three of them laughing and carrying on, making big-butt jokes. It seemed both out of and in character for their mother. It was a side of her they sensed—the girlfriend—but that they hadn't seen much, having forced her into the stodgy role of mother all their lives, the keeper of rules, the enforcer, the enculturator of little girls. But here she was, cutting loose, her true jokey self. A memory Miriam would relish forever.

They pulled up in front of Jackson-Wilkens. Miriam had brought a camera. She wanted to record the momentous occasion. She also wanted a reminder of her mother's black and blue face, in case she forgot, further down the road, why this day was necessary. Linda posed with their mother, then Miriam. Miriam felt a little deceitful. She knew her mother would not want her picture taken if she remembered how she looked. But she didn't remember. She smiled into the camera, unsuspecting.

The social worker met them in the lobby. (*See how nice this is, Mother—isn't this furniture beautiful, and look at that lovely old grandfather's clock.* I used to have a clock like that, didn't I? their mother asked. Where is that clock? *Linda has it!*) She took them to the lounge on the second floor, across from their mother's new room. The charge nurse, Margie, would do the intake. Their mother gracious, cooperative, calm. How could this be going so well? It was going better than Miriam could ever have imagined. This wasn't so hard, after all!

Intake consisted of numerous questions about their mother and her care requirements. They filled out forms, worked up a care sheet, noted preferences, special needs, went through medications, very thorough. Margie chatted amiably, friendly as could be. Their mother sat dignified in her wheelchair, trying to answer when she could but deferring to Miriam most of the time. She couldn't remember what her needs were exactly. Just the ordinary ones, Miriam thought: to be loved, cared for, secure, safe. Nothing extraordinary, really.

Finally the intake was over. Miriam could tell that her mother was worn out. It had been a long day. They wheeled her across the hall to "her" room, not that there was anything in there that was hers. The single bed, which Miriam and Linda had made up last night with a new spread from Target, the institutional chest of drawers and bedside table, the arm chair with its straight back and wooden arms, and of course, a linoleum floor. Miriam and Linda would meet Ted at The Kensington later this afternoon, to collect her La-Z-Boy rocker and personal things.

"See the nice view of the lake," Linda said to her mother. "Remember how we looked at this room yesterday?"

But no, her mother didn't remember. And now a frown was forming on her face. Suddenly Miriam understood that her mother hadn't gotten it at all. She didn't understand that now she would be living here. That they would be leaving her here. She might have understood at moments, in some ways. But she hadn't understood at all in the big way, the real way. She was looking up at Miriam and Linda with the expectation that now she'd leave with them: three girlfriends out on a lark. But the lark was over.

"So this is where you'll be living now, Mother," Linda said, in that cajoling voice she used to try to make everything all right with their mother. "Margie will look after you. We'll be back in a little while with your blue chair—remember your blue La-Z-Boy?—and your things."

"You mean I'm supposed to stay here?" their mother asked in a bewildered voice. "You're going to leave me here?"

Miriam felt the blood leave her body.

"I don't want to stay here!" their mother wailed. "I want to go home!" She began to weep bitter, bitter tears. Right before her very eyes, Miriam saw her mother's heart break. And at that moment, her own heart broke too.

Home, home, home ... I want to go home! The words echoed in Miriam's mind as she and Linda—criminals, murderers—crept down the hall and away.

Home ... home ... home ...

But their mother was home.

Lost Lake

Miriam Batson's mother had been living in the nursing home for exactly one year in August. For the first six months, Miriam wasn't sure either of them would live through it. Not that her mother was failing physically or dying, any more than usual. She was fine, physically, if you consider not being able to walk or remember "fine." The nurses there were even able to "train her bowels," as they put it, conjuring up some strange images in Miriam's mind. The only medications she took were vitamins, an aspirin a day, and St. John's Wort. (Miriam's suggestion; she began taking it too).

When her mother first moved into Jackson-Wilkens, Miriam was careful never to use the term "nursing home," always referring to it as "the residence" or "where you live now." But a week or so after she moved in, when Miriam and her husband Ted were visiting, Ted "blurted out" (in Miriam's opinion), "So, how do you like the nursing home so far?" Miriam had sent him such a blistering look that later they had remarked on it and laughed. "I knew I was in trouble," Ted said. "I just didn't know why." Miriam's mother seemed unfazed, though even with the ice broken, Miriam herself still couldn't use the term around her mother.

Until, that is, one day about a month later, when her mother was complaining as usual about how she didn't have any help, how she didn't know how much longer she could go on living on her own, and Miriam, exasperated, asked, "Well, Mother, where do you think you should be living?" Her mother piped right up, "In a nursing home." Miriam, astonished and abashed, exclaimed before she could stop herself, "But Mother, this is a nursing home!" Then she stammered, "A really nice one, of course, a really *nice* nursing home ..." When her mother didn't object, it occurred to Miriam that maybe she was actually relieved. It was Miriam who couldn't take it.

The social worker at Jackson-Wilkens had told Miriam that the adjustment to the nursing home could take from three months to a year, and of course she had been referring to Miriam's mother's adjustment. But Miriam came to see that her own adjustment was going to take that long, if not forever. Where her mother's care was concerned, she was either in a rage or depressed or as grateful as a dog who prostrates itself in a servile position to show how unworthy it is, how needy, how unbearably happy to have a kind word or deed. Miriam supposed she passed for normal, didn't appear to be a mental case coming and going (often), but she seethed with emotions, caught up in micromanaging everything from her mother's laundry (she did it herself, after the residence laundry lost two pajama bottoms) to her mother's so-called social life (taking her mother to "wine" and cheese, conversing animatedly with anyone who could still hear and even those who couldn't). She had nighttime dreams of springing her mother from the nursing home, as if it were a prison to which her mother had been sentenced for life, which, in a way, she had.

No, her mother wasn't about to die, and neither was

Miriam, except in some subtle, hard-to-explain ways. But it was a hard adjustment for them both. For the first few weeks, her mother was really angry, angry and confused. She still had Miriam's telephone number at that point (and three phones in her room, so she wouldn't have to get up to answer and risk falling), and she'd call in the evening, "sundowning," as the nurses called it, irrational, unreasonable, blaming, accusing, really ugly: "Why have you done this to me? You wouldn't treat a dog this way! Come get me! Take me home! I can't believe you'd do this to your own mother!" and so on and so forth. Hard to listen to. Hard to argue with. And of course the next day she wouldn't remember.

But gradually things began to get better. Miriam got to know the nurses and aides, and began to trust them to do their jobs. The routine and regularity of the nursing home was good for her mother, though she never knew, day to day, what would happen next. Someone took her to meals three times a day, every day, in her wheelchair. Although her mother could not remember this, Miriam could, which counted for something. By summer her mother seemed content more days than not, and on an even keel most of the time. She even began to participate a bit in activities, which was something she had balked at for the first many months. A couple of times that summer Miriam called and her mother was as happy and breathless as an excited girl: "You'll never guess where I've been today!"

"Where?"

"Spartanburg. Those girls I know in the Garden Club invited me to go. We saw the most beautiful gardens and all those beautiful homes around Spartanburg, and then we had lunch out." Her mother was laughing, pleased with herself.

Never mind that Spartanburg was in South Carolina, about thirty miles from Greenville, where her mother had lived until Miriam moved her to Minneapolis. Miriam had gotten very good at extrapolating what she thought of as "the truth." The recreation therapists had taken a busload of residents for a ride, probably around the chain of lakes. Her mother had translated this into the garden club, Spartanburg, and lunch out, though Miriam was almost 100 percent sure they had returned to the nursing home in time for lunch. Though who's to say? Maybe her mother had been to Spartanburg that day.

"What a wonderful thing to do!" Miriam exclaimed.

It was a very beautiful summer, and many afternoons Miriam wheeled her mother outside to the front patio of the nursing home, which had a wrought-iron picnic table with an umbrella and some comfortable patio chairs. She sat with her mother, enjoying the day: temperature in the eighties, low humidity, fresh air, the comings and goings of people from the nursing home, the big oaks in front, green grass. Special treats included seeing a crow land on the lawn, or a plane pass over. Her mother was quite attuned to the sound of airplanes, which Miriam had grown accustomed to and hardly noticed anymore. But her mother, as soon as she heard the far-away roar, would begin scanning the skies, hoping to see the plane. Those were pleasant times, peaceful times, and Miriam would marvel that they had landed safely themselves, after a long, bumpy, difficult flight.

Perhaps it was summer itself that prompted thoughts of getting away. Often when they sat out front on a gorgeous summer day, her mother would ask Miriam, "When are we going to the mountains?" One didn't really go to mountains in Minnesota, but that was beside the point. Miriam understood what her mother was saying: *When are we going on vacation?* When, her mother was asking, are we going to indulge in the pleasure of plans and anticipation, when do we get to pack, when do we load the car and take off, when do we get to a simpler place, a cabin where all we have to do is sweep, when are we going to kick back and eat pimento cheese sandwiches in our bathing suits for lunch, when are we going to stay up late playing bridge, when are we going to get away from our regular, humdrum lives and have some fun? *When are we going to the mountains?*

Good question! Miriam had begun asking herself the same thing. She and Ted hadn't had a vacation themselves that summer. Ted was a solo attorney, so there was no one to look after his practice when he was out of town, Miriam was teaching part-time, and of course there was her mother to look after. Miriam found her thoughts roaming to former summer vacations, especially those when she was a child. She felt, grumpily, that to be grown up was to forgo pleasure in some fundamental way. Joy, when she was a child, had come from what she thought of as "the elements": sun, water, sand. She remembered being surrounded by people all the time, her parents, sister, cousins, and aunts and uncles, both actual and honorary. The past seemed bright, crowded, exciting, just one wonderful treat after another.

Of course that wasn't right. Her childhood and youth weren't completely fun. Think about school. Think about practicing piano. Think about avoiding her mother's displeasure. Think about loneliness, excruciating shyness, boredom, self-consciousness, unconsciousness.

Still, they had their share of good times, especially at the cabin. After school was out in early June, they moved to their cabin near Table Rock State Park, in the foothills of the Blue Ridge Mountains, thirty miles north of Greenville. Her father commuted to his radio and TV store in downtown Greenville every day. Their mother drove Miriam and Linda to the state park beach, where they spent their days sunning and swimming in Table Rock Lake. In the evenings, Miriam's mother and father rocked and talked in the dark on the big screen porch. Miriam would lie in perfect contentment in the Pawley's Island hammock, while the katydids in the woods all around them filled up the night with sound.

So Miriam knew what her mother was after when she asked when were they going to the mountains. It was the natural, necessary thing to get away. She knew how much her mother would love to go to a cabin. She wanted to go there with her, to try to recapture some of that pleasure that seemed just out of reach.

Last summer, she and Linda tried to take their mother to a cabin. Miriam researched handicapped-accessible places and rented a log cabin overlooking Lake Superior for three days at the end of August, when Linda would be in Minnesota. But right before they were to leave, her mother fell several times, hurting her leg and bruising her whole face. Those falls precipitated the move from assisted living into the nursing home. Instead of taking their mother to a cabin as they had planned, Linda and Miriam spent the vacation moving her to Jackson-Wilkens. And then the long, difficult months of adjustment for both Miriam and her mother.

But now, a year later, her mother was getting along so well, maybe Miriam could take her to a cabin this summer. A juxtaposition rose in her mind: on the one hand, the nursing home, with its linoleum floors, three shifts of nurses and aides, the occasional weeping or yelling of some demented resident, the meals eaten mainly in silence with strangers, the endless hours spent alone, the loneliness. On the other hand, a cabin. Sunny days on the deck, meals eaten with people you loved, the silence of woods at night, open windows and cool air for sleeping in a real bed (not the single, institutional bed her mother had been reduced to), a lake shining blue through a stand of birch.

"When are we going to the mountains?" her mother asked. She sounded pleading, Miriam thought.

"People don't really go to the mountains in Minnesota, Mother. They go to the lake."

"Well, when are we going to the lake?"

"I'm looking into it."

As indeed she was. This lake couldn't be too far away, and the cabin had to be handicapped accessible. Grab bars for sure. Not so easy to find.

Then a friend mentioned a resort about two and a half hours from the Twin Cities where her family went every year. Lost Lake Lodge. As soon as Miriam got the brochure, as soon as she saw its green, leafy cover with pictures of split-log cabins and decks facing a lake, she wanted to go. She wanted to go, and she wanted to take her mother.

She called right away. Lost Lake Lodge had a one-bedroom, handicapped-accessible cabin, at $300 a night for the three of them, for Miriam would have to take Ted. "Take" him, for he wouldn't exactly want to go. Going to a cabin with Miriam's mother was not Ted's idea of a vacation. But Miriam needed him. She couldn't lift the wheelchair in and out of the car by herself, plus she needed him to be there for her. $300 seemed a lot for a night at a cabin, but it included breakfast and dinner at the lodge, and Miriam, gaining momentum, disregarded expense. Her mother would pay for half of it from the dwindling funds Miriam managed. It was exactly the kind of place she longed to go to and take her mother. She reserved it for four nights at the end of August.

"Four nights!" Ted exclaimed. "Isn't that a little long?" He left "to be with your mother?" unspoken, but understood.

"But why go if we can't really get away and relax?" Miriam asked. "Anything else seems too short." She didn't mention that she really wanted to go for a week.

Her mind was filled with fantasies of the great time they'd have at Lost Lake. How wonderful it would be, like old times … or if not old times exactly … because, after all, her mother was old and couldn't remember diddly-squat … and granted, she needed a lot of caretaking. But she was still able to enjoy things, she still wanted to go to the mountains! Miriam could take care of her for a few days, couldn't she? Four days wasn't that long.

"Four days is way too long," her friend Ellen told her at their weekly support group. The support group, "for friends and relatives of loved ones at Jackson-Wilkins," was actually a support trio: Miriam; Ellen, who took care of her grandmother; and Joyce. Like Miriam, Joyce took care of her mother. Unlike Miriam, Joyce came to the nursing home twice a day to hand feed her mother. The next winter, both these old ladies would die within a month of one another. End of support group. Well, it had been good while it lasted.

Ellen, who had more experience caretaking than Miriam, had tried taking her grandmother to the family cabin one year. "It about killed me," Ellen said. "I couldn't leave her alone for long. I had to sleep in the room with her and get up a zillion times during the night because she was always having to pee. Plus it didn't matter to her whether we were there or not. She was long past being able to enjoy it. We came home early."

Miriam was taken aback. She couldn't imagine cutting short their vacation.

"Do yourself a favor," Ellen said. "Make it two nights. Your mother won't know the difference."

"I think she's right," Joyce said.

Miriam went home and changed the reservation to two nights. She'd always found Ellen's advice on the money, and Miriam had to admit she had trouble spending two hours around her mother, answering a million questions over and over. But why not play it safe? And why put Ted through four days of her mother?

Finally, the big day arrived. It was a Sunday late in August, a beautiful day with temperatures in the seventies, after two days of thunderstorms and torrential rains. The weather seemed a good omen. Miriam and Ted packed the car, which didn't take long, as they were only going for two nights. They couldn't bring much, given the room they'd need in the car for her mother's things: her wheelchair, which would take up the whole back of their small station wagon; the portable bed rail that slipped under a mattress and couldn't be folded to a smaller size; her mother's suitcase, which Miriam had packed the day before; her rolling walker; and of course the port-a-potty, a bulky contraption with a bucket that they'd need to place next to her mother's bed at night. Miriam feared they might have to tie it on top of the car.

For several weeks, ever since Miriam made the reservations, she had enjoyed answering her mother's query about going to the mountains with some specific plans and an actual date. She'd shown her mother the brochure over and over. It wasn't clear if her mother could remember that they were going on a little trip, though sometimes it seemed that she did. Miriam was so used to prompting her mother, filling in for her, faking that she was holding up her end of a conversation, that Miriam wasn't sure, really, what she supplied and what came from her mother. She pondered how unpredictable her mother's memory was, storing some things and erasing others, without too much rhyme or reason. Sometimes her mother was uncannily with it, her old self, and other times she couldn't compute a thing.

On the morning they were to leave, Miriam called her mother at Jackson-Wilkens to tell her she and Ted would be over to get her after lunch. But her mother had forgotten about the trip; it was news to her. "What a nice surprise! Are ya'll sure you want to take me? I don't want to be a bother." When they arrived, she was dressed in the periwinkle blue, matching knit pants and top Miriam had put out for the aide. Miriam finished up her mother's suitcase. At the elevator, the nurses and aides gathered around her in her wheelchair, wishing her a good time, telling her to behave. A resident going on a vacation wasn't the usual thing. Other residents sitting around in their wheelchairs seemed to eye her mother with envy, though Miriam was never sure how much most of them understood. She cut her eyes at them guiltily, her heart twisting. *I wish I could take you, too.*

Oh, it was a dream come true! A beautiful summer day, everything loaded in the car (even the port-a-potty) and her mother buckled in the back seat, thrilled to be going to the mountains at last. They were gone by one-thirty, right on schedule, and the drive went fine. Her mother didn't even have to go to the bathroom the whole way, much to Miriam's relief, for that would have necessitated unpacking enough to get the wheelchair out. And she stayed awake, much to Miriam's surprise, enjoying the scenery. They pulled into Lost Lake Lodge about four o'clock.

The cabin was everything Miriam could have asked for, a golden honey color with a fireplace and nice furniture inside. After they'd unloaded, they all sat on the deck, her mother in her wheelchair and Ted and Miriam in deck chairs. Miriam got out the cheese and crackers and had a ginger ale with her mother while Ted had a beer. It was just the way she'd imagined, everything she'd wanted, the beautiful lake down the hill through the whispering, silvery green leaves of the birches, the late summer day with just a touch of fall in the air, her mother at a cabin again, relaxing on the deck.

But after a little while, Miriam noticed that her mother had gotten very quiet. She hadn't said anything in maybe ten minutes, and Miriam asked her if she was feeling all right. Suddenly she looked exhausted and complained of being sick to her stomach, dizzy. Even though she was sitting up in her wheelchair, there was a definite sense that she had melted down.

Miriam, alarmed, wheeled her into the bedroom and helped her into bed.

"I feel sick," her mother said. "I think y'all better take me home now."

Home! They'd just gotten there!

"Maybe you're just tired, Mother," Miriam tried. "It's been a big day. Why don't you just lie here and shut your eyes for a bit, and then you'll feel better."

"Who would ever have believed I'd act this way!" her mother berated herself.

"What way, Mother?"

Her mother seemed confused. "I don't know. Getting sick."

"You're not sick, Mother. You're just tired. Try to rest now."

Miriam shut the door part way and went out to the deck. Ted raised his eyebrows at her in a question. "I think she's just tired," Miriam said, "and maybe anxious." Her own anxiety level was sky high.

It was almost time to go over to the lodge for dinner. Miriam hadn't brought any groceries, because their breakfasts and dinners were included at the lodge. They could order lunch there, which Miriam planned to do. She let her mother rest for twenty minutes more, but then they needed to go, before it got too late.

"Ya'll go without me," her mother said. "Can't ya'll just bring something back over here for me?"

Miriam felt her stomach knot up. What was going on? She had a feeling her mother was just tired, disoriented. Maybe she was hungry, needed something more to eat. They'd have to go to the lodge for dinner. Miriam got her up, into the wheelchair, and Ted rolled her to the car. They'd drive the short way to the lodge. Maybe she'd feel better when she ate something. Miriam's head felt tight, as if someone were pinching the neck muscles at the base of her skull.

The lodge dining room was knotty pine, with a view of Lost Lake. The tables had white cloths and little yellow lanterns, and the menu was Northwood-sy, with walleye pike and sirloin steak. Indeed, her mother rallied. She ate some of her salad and a bit of her dinner, the most she ever ate, and Ted (bless his heart) entertained her with stories of his youth, spent at his grandfather's cabin in northern Wisconsin.

"We've been coming to this place for fifty years," her mother told him. "We came last year, but someone already had our cabin so we didn't stay."

"Ah," Ted said. "Well, it sure is a nice place."

"Do you want dessert, Mother?" Miriam asked when the waitress appeared to clear their table. "Maybe some ice cream?"

Her mother ate every bite of the ice cream, and Miriam began to feel that maybe things would be okay. "Back on track," she said to Ted, as he loaded the wheelchair into the car after dinner. "This is harder than I thought."

At the cabin she went through the ritual of getting her mother ready for bed, helping her undress and get into her pajamas, cleaning her face with cleansing cream, brushing her teeth, pulling down her pants so she could pee. She and Ted stuck the portable bed rail under the mattress of the double bed in the bedroom. Miriam would sleep next to her mother in the single bed, and Ted on the fold-out Murphy bed in the living room. "I'm sorry," Miriam mouthed to him.

Finally her mother was in bed. Only she was cold and fretting. Miriam found another blanket. She was exhausted herself, but sat out in the living room with Ted for a while, trying to read with both ears cocked to the bedroom. What if her mother tried to get up, what if she fell? She'd break something for sure, a hip or arm, and then where would they be? "It'll be okay," Ted said. "She's an old woman. She's not able to handle much any more."

"How come I keep forgetting that?"

When Miriam went into the bedroom to check on her, her mother was breathing deeply. Asleep, good. But suddenly she let out a blood-curdling scream, almost stopping Miriam's heart, and sat up in bed.

"It's just me, Mother," Miriam said quickly, going over and sitting on the side of the bed, taking her cold hand. "We're at the cabin and you've been asleep."

Her mother looked at her groggily in the half-light from the bathroom. "I thought a stranger was in the room."

"Just me," Miriam soothed. "Now go to sleep." Her own nerves were still jangling, as if she were a bell that had been struck. Quietly Miriam put on her nightgown and got into the single bed. But in just a little while, as she was about to drift off, she sensed that her mother was sitting up on the side of the bed, about to topple forward. Miriam leaped up.

"I have to pee."

Miriam had put the port-a-potty right by the bed. She helped her sidle over to it, using the walker. Her mother couldn't even stand on her own anymore. She reminded Miriam of a loon, graceful and agile in the water but unable to maneuver on land. Her mother was definitely out of her element, not only here at the cabin, Miriam thought sadly, but everywhere now.

Miriam reached behind her mother and pulled down her pajamas. She had to bend over a bit to do this, which put her face near her mother's butt.

Back to bed. All through the night, eight or ten times, Miriam gave up counting, she would hear a slight movement and there would be her mother, sitting on the side of the bed, about to get up on her own. She wouldn't say anything, no warning, so Miriam had to be alert and ready. She lay stiff and terrified that her mother would try to get up and fall. Back at the nursing home there was an alarm, an electric eye on a pole. If her mother rose from her bed, the alarm would go off, alerting someone to come. But Miriam had declined to bring the alarm, figuring they shouldn't have an alarm going off at night in the woods, disturbing other guests nearby.

How could anyone pee so many times? If she hadn't been checked, Miriam would think her mother had a bladder infection.

Once Miriam fell asleep for a few minutes, long enough to dream that Linda had come to town and sold their mother's house for $75,000, without asking Miriam or consulting with anyone about the market value. She even arranged for their mother to go to Cleveland (Cleveland? A town they had no connection with) to visit a friend, and when she came back, Miriam was supposed to find her a place to live. Miriam was furious! She screamed at Linda, "You asshole!" Then Linda and she had a "difference of opinion" about their mother. Linda said that their mother did much better around her, "she's just a sweetheart," and that she was more needy and dependent around Miriam. Then there was a sad, tender part where Miriam was cradling her mother, comforting her. The dream skipped to Miriam trying to help her mother cross a busy street, how would they ever get across, and on the other side was an incline, with steps, which they'd have to climb …

Miriam woke with a start. Her mother was sitting on the side of the bed.

Morning at last. Ah, morning. Miriam's mother was cold. She had gotten hot during the night, and Miriam had turned back the extra blanket. Now she was freezing, miserable. "I can't believe how I'm spoiling y'all's fun," her mother said. "I don't want to be a burden."

But she was a burden, that much was clear. Miriam was beginning to grasp, at more than an intellectual level, why there were three shifts at the nursing home. She felt bleary-eyed and fatigued from lack of sleep, as if she'd been clubbed, and the day stretched out before her like a huge expanse of terrain she had to trek. She went into the living room and got into the Murphy bed next to Ted, who was just waking from a great night's sleep.

"I think we should leave after breakfast," Miriam whispered. "I didn't get any sleep, and I don't think she's even enjoying it all that much. I don't think I can take another night like last night."

"Aw, baby," Ted said, pulling her close. "I'm sorry. Maybe you don't have to decide right now. See how she does at breakfast."

She helped her mother into the bathroom to pee, get dressed, and do hair, teeth, lipstick. "I bet you haven't gotten any rest," her mother said. She was always quick to assess Miriam's physical state, and Miriam looked as if she'd been up all night, which she had. "I didn't get much sleep," she said. Her mother: "What'd you have to do?"

They loaded her and the wheelchair into the car, went to the lodge for breakfast, came back to the cabin. It was only ten o'clock. She deposited her mother in a rocking chair in the living room with a view of Lost Lake, and there she simply sat. Nothing to do, just like the nursing home. She didn't seem interested in the view of the lake. Finally Miriam gave her the front page of the *New York Times*, which they'd brought from home, and that seemed to satisfy her. She actually looked through it, maybe read something? Unlikely, with her double vision, but maybe she looked at the pictures.

She used to enjoy the Sunday paper at home in Greenville. After Miriam moved away, she was frustrated by the Sunday paper when she was home, so thin, over so quickly, nothing to read. But her parents could make a whole morning of it, sitting in their La-Z-Boy rockers. Miriam saw just a shadow of that now, though her mother was bundled up in a heavy shirt with a wool blanket over her legs.

At Ted's suggestion, he and Miriam walked around Lost Lake. It wasn't a very big lake, but it was connected to a huge expanse of water by a channel and a bridge. There was a nice woodland trail, but Miriam was nervous about leaving her mother. "She seemed to do fine at breakfast," Ted said. "Maybe we should stick it out."

Miriam stared at the lake, so blue and fresh in the morning. She felt ragged and irritable. "Well, we might as well stay through lunch," she said.

She decided to lie down for a little while when they got back to the cabin. Her mother seemed set for the moment, maybe about to nod off herself. She did sleep a lot at the nursing home. As soon as Miriam hit the bed, she was asleep. But maybe ten minutes into her nap, she heard a familiar voice from the living room: "Is anybody out there?" Her mother meant the deck, where Ted was reading. He and Miriam answered simultaneously. "I have to go to the bathroom," her mother said, "and I'm wondering how I'm going to do that." Miriam rose from her nap. She must have a bladder the size of a pea.

When Miriam pushed her wheelchair into the bedroom to get to the bathroom, her mother said, "Is this where you slept?"

"And you," Miriam told her.

Her mother looked around her. Miriam pointed out the bed she had slept in. But her mother had never seen it before.

"Where's the bathroom?" her mother said in a worried voice. It had taken her all year to recognize her room at the nursing home, and there were still days when it was unfamiliar to her. Every time she returned from the beauty parlor on her floor, she told Miriam, "I've just been here one day, you know, so I don't really know what to expect." There were so many things to process every day that her mother couldn't manage. Miriam couldn't imagine what that was like—each moment new, maybe scary, nothing familiar.

"I'm going to tell the manager to prepare our bill," Miriam told Ted on the deck. "We'll leave after lunch."

"Are you sure?"

"I don't think I can take another sleepless night. It's not worth it. It's just too much for her."

"If that's the way you feel," Ted said.

"Oh I just don't know!" Miriam said.

They were the only ones in the dining room at lunch, as most people brought their own sandwich makings. Out the window came the sounds of children playing in the swimming area, the occasional clunk of a boat coming into the dock, or a motor starting up. All the lovely summer sounds of a day at the lake.

Her mother seemed fine, really, as fine as she ever was. Observing her, Miriam thought that no one who encountered her briefly—the waitress for example—would be able to tell that anything but old age was wrong with her mother. She compensated so well when she had to, in public, deferring to Miriam or Ted if she had trouble with any questions. Ted was so nice to her, helping her order, something her mother was no longer capable of doing. ("I'll have whatever you're having.") But Miriam knew better. Her mother got by on a lifetime accumulation of coherency, but she could only keep it up for so long. All Miriam could do was be kind to her, to try to anticipate what would make her the least anxious and ill at ease.

Miriam got up and went in to tell the manager to prepare their bill, so they could leave after lunch. But as soon as she went into the lobby, with its stone fireplace and bird's nest on the mantle, she couldn't do it. She lost her resolve. She hated to cut the vacation short! She had wanted to do this so much! How could she leave after only one night! If they left now, her mother would never go to the mountains again.

Miriam fled, following the flagstones that formed a path down to the lake. She walked out on an old abandoned dock, beyond the swimming area. She felt like flinging herself into the lake, sinking like a stone to the bottom. If they left now, her mother would never again sleep in a cabin. Never again sit on a deck overlooking a lake. Never again feel the pleasure of a vacation. All of that would be over for her. It already was.

Miriam lay down on the dock, feeling the weight of her heart, how it sank down, down, down into the dark, the cold. She was so tired! It felt as if she had been struggling for years—well, the three years she'd been taking care of her mother. She had bailed and bailed, but still her mother was sinking. If only she could rest a moment ... The worn wood of the dock felt so soothing, so warm. She shut her eyes. Summer days, lost lakes, memories, her mother, everything flowed together in the soothing murmur of water all around her. For some timeless time she floated there, neither asleep nor awake. Maybe dying wasn't so bad after all. After the long struggle, the holding on. But then the letting go ... The sense of being held up, received.

Miriam opened her eyes. How blue the sky was, a whole lake itself! The blue of memory, the blue of forgetting, a whole blue lake of eternity, where nothing ever ended, nothing was ever lost. She thought of her dead and felt them to be with her. They floated through her memory like beautiful white clouds.

Miriam got up and went back to the dining room. Her mother had eaten a whole half of her sandwich, and she and Ted were carrying on a normal conversation. Ted was doing most of the talking, but her mother was clearly entertained, enjoying herself.

"Can we get them to wrap this for us?" her mother asked Miriam about the other half of her sandwich. She always wanted to take a doggy bag home, couldn't bear to leave good food on her plate.

"Sure," Miriam said. When the waitress came, Miriam said, "Could you wrap that for my mother to take, and would you tell the manager to prepare our bill? We'll be leaving this afternoon."

Ted looked at her in surprise. "I thought ... "

"That was then," Miriam said. "This is now." The now and the now and the now. That was the mantra her yoga teacher intoned sometimes, until the words blurred into nothingness, leaving them suspended in time, not past, not future, not even the present as Miriam usually thought of it, but in that other dimension—the now.

It was not as if the trip was a terrible mistake. It was that it was too late. Her mother could no longer do this sort of thing. Miriam couldn't do it. Now they'd concentrate on what was left. They'd sit outside Jackson-Wilkens and watch the planes fly overhead. She'd take her mother to wine and cheese on Wednesday afternoons. There were still things left. Pulling down her mother's pants, that would certainly go on. The falls would go on. Cutting a fresh nectarine and giving her mother slices would go on. What they had left, what they had together, now. What was not yet lost.

Her mother accepted that they were leaving that afternoon without questions. She couldn't remember, after all, how long they had been there—a day or a month. But she got confused and fretful in the car on the way back.

"Where did y'all leave your car?"

"This is our car, Mother."

"Then where's my car?"

"You don't have one anymore."

Indignant: "I don't?"

"You're eighty-seven years old. You don't drive anymore."

"Well, I could hire someone!"

Later: "Miriam, do I have any help?"

"There are three shifts of nurses and aides where you live."

"Where do I live?"

"In Jackson-Wilkens," Miriam said. She paused. "The nursing home."

Silence from the backseat, as her mother absorbed this.

"Well, we had a wonderful trip," she said. And then,

"What day is this?"

"Monday."

"So that cabin rented from Monday to Monday."

"Right."

Miriam turned on the radio. She was beginning to feel barraged with questions, and she was jagged from lack of sleep. The questions always had a tinge of anxiety, which Miriam found catching, or were totally confused, which made her sad, or were a bit belligerent, as if she and Ted were trying to put something over on her. All Miriam wanted was to get back to the nursing home.

"Boy," Ted said as they neared the Twin Cities. "The traffic is really picking up!"

"That's Greenville," her mother said.

Of course the nurses were surprised—though not too surprised, Miriam noticed—to see them back.

"Is this where I live?" her mother said, looking around, trying to place herself.

"Yes it is, Mother. You've lived here for a year. See your big La-Z-Boy and those hideous pictures of Linda and me when we were in high school?"

"I don't think they're hideous," her mother said. "When will you be back?"

"Tomorrow," Miriam said, "I'll be back tomorrow." Though she was already thinking of taking the day off.

"What will I do about dinner?"

"Someone will come take you in your wheelchair."

"Are you sure?"

"I'm 100 percent sure."

Her mother looked skeptical. "All right," she said. Then she said, "I love you, Miriam."

Miriam paused in the doorway to behold her mother,

whom she knew so well that she hardly saw her most of the time. So that was it, really. That was what it all came down to in the end. Something so simple, really.

"I love you too," Miriam said.

Unforgettable

Nat King Cole's warm, velvety voice croons "Unforgettable" from the tape deck in Miriam's car. She's playing the most mellow music she could find, hoping it will help her relax. Around her on I-94, it's snowing like crazy. A straight-line wind from the west—the direction she's driving—pushes the snow fiercely against her windshield. She has the wiper blades on high, but they can hardly keep up. It wasn't snowing when she left the Twin Cities about half an hour ago, but as soon as she cleared the city limits, as soon as she hit open country, the snow materialized. She can barely see the back end of the truck in front of her. She really doesn't want to have to turn back now.

Funny, "Unforgettable" is the name of the capital campaign to remodel Jackson-Wilkins, the nursing home where her mother lives. Miriam laughed ruefully the first time she heard the name—a lot of the residents at Jackson-Wilkens can't remember a thing. How long has her mother lived there? Will it be two or three years this August?

Miriam can't remember. She can't remember when it was that she moved her mother to Minnesota from South Carolina—was that three or four years ago last February? Her mother can't remember what day it is, what week it is, what month, year, century, millennium. Miriam wonders if she's heading in the same direction.

It wasn't snowing at all when she left her Italian lesson at two-thirty. Today they worked on going shopping. *"Vorrei quattro panini."* It's the *aglis, deglis, daglis, suglis and neglis* that get her. Not to mention masculine and feminine nouns, pronouns, adjectives, and possessives. The snow is really beating against … *la finestra.* Feminine. She doesn't know many words. She's a wildly enthusiastic but mediocre student of Italian. She has no ear for it and she'll never master *chi, che, ce, ci. Non è possible.* Thank goodness some of the words are *similare* to *Inglese.*

She's always wanted to speak a foreign language. She took French in high school and for two years in college but never with any enjoyment. She got off on the wrong foot because she was so intimidated—bullied, really— by her high-school French teacher. Mr. Montgomery. He seemed bent on making his students feel like hicks, which they were. Whenever her school bus was late, a rather frequent occurrence, Monsieur Montgomery (what kind of French name is Montgomery?) would pounce on her as soon as she came in the door, self-conscious, blushing, late. He'd fire off rapid, incomprehensible, accusing questions: *"Pourquoi êtes-vous en retard, Mademoiselle Batson?"* He ruined French for her forever.

But now she's over fifty and a beginning Italian student. *Mi chiama Miriam Batson.* It gives her no end of pleasure to be able to say anything in Italian—even the simplest, easiest things. *Buon giorno*, she says now, in the car, to the snow. She can't think how to say *stop*. Isn't learning something new supposed to strengthen your memory? Give it a good workout? When exactly is she actually going to start lifting those pathetic little free weights (one pound, two) in the basement? Strong women stay young!

She starts the song over, soothed by Nat's mellow voice. "Unforgettable." So says the huge banner across the front of Jackson-Wilkens. The remodeling—which has been going on for almost a year now and is costing *molti milioni* dollars—has involved so much demolition, dust, drilling, disruption and—Miriam sometimes thinks to herself, death—that it's proving to be unforgettable in ways the planners never dreamed of.

Today, for example, when she stopped by before leaving town, she felt she was entering a bombed-out building in Dresden. The "Unforgettable" project had reached ground zero. The whole lobby was gutted, with plywood partitions set up to keep the residents from harm's way. There was a makeshift reception desk in one area, and silver heating ducts and pipes exposed in the open ceiling. Walls had been knocked out, and what was left of the carpet was worn and stained with splatters of plaster.

Miriam did note, however, a new development: mailboxes for the assisted-living residents had been installed in the back wall. The idea was that the main floor would be like Main Street in a small town, where you could greet your neighbors, pick up your mail, go shopping at the little gift shop, buy a cup of coffee and a cookie at the "cafe." It was going to be great—but in the meantime— unforgettable.

• • •

Snowing! And it's April 12, for Pete's sake. Who is Pete? St. Peter? She doesn't want to say "for God's sake," or worse, "for Christ's sake," because she's on her way to a monastery. Not that she's Catholic. She doesn't know much about Catholicism first-hand, just what she's learned from what Catholics, practicing and recovering, have told her. She's gotten the feeling that she doesn't want to know too much more.

The temperature on the car thermometer says it's thirty-two degrees outside. It was forty-seven degrees when she left her Italian lesson. Maybe she's driving right into a front. She turns off the tape, turns on the radio to get the weather. "Snowing lightly in St. Cloud," someone says. Lightly! Obviously they're not driving in it. How far is she from St. Cloud? What a lovely name—she's never given it a thought before. Now the snow is actually sticking and making the grass—what's left of it after winter—white. Easter is next week. Isn't it supposed to be spring?

She starts the tape over. "Unforgettable ..." She saw one of the workmen she knew this afternoon when she stopped by Jackson-Wilkens, one of the ones who had gotten to know her mother when he was working on the second floor, her mother's floor. *How's it going? How's your mom doing?* That sort of thing. Pleasant. The workmen have been around so long now, they seem like a permanent fixture themselves. But nothing is really permanent at Jackson-Wilkens. Least of all the residents.

Some of the workmen got to know her mother a little too well when they were working on her floor. She was the old lady screaming in the hall. Begging them to help her escape. *I want to go home!* Miriam's face burns at the thought of it. Her actual mother, whose credo in life was *Never make a scene, never make anyone uncomfortable.* Sometimes the nurses would call Miriam, and she could hear her mother yelling all the way to the nurses' station. Yelling and screaming, completely out of control. Unforgettable.

She passes the exit for St. Cloud. Thank goodness she knows where she is now. Easter. She's not sure what she and her husband Ted will do. They're not very religious. Going to church only on the big occasions—Christmas, Easter—seems pretty bogus. They're not what you'd call faithful.

Easters when she was growing up … They'd always go to church, of course. Earle Street Baptist. Hats were a big part of Easter. New spring dresses in pastel colors, patent leather shoes, a pretty pocketbook, and a hat to finish off the outfit. They went through a lot of beautiful Easter frocks over the years: organdy, polished cotton, linen. A lavender dotted-swiss dress with a full skirt and lace trim floats into her mind. Their mother always bought good clothes for Miriam and her sister, Linda, when they were growing up. Greenville had several exclusive women's shops, as well as a couple of good department stores— Ivy's, Meyers-Arnold—on Main Street, where her father had his radio and TV business. People would walk down Main Street, greet each other, run into friends. Buy a cup of coffee at Woolworth's. Miriam remembers going into Woolworth's as a child with her mother to see Neva, the maid who had cared for Miriam and Linda when they were little. Neva had gotten a job behind the soda counter. That was before blacks could sit at the counter themselves. Where is Neva now?

She must be getting near the exit for St. John's Monastery, though she's a little afraid she'll miss the green highway sign in the snow. The visibility is really poor. She made this reservation at the monastery guesthouse two months ago. She had looked forward to being there in the spring.

She e-mailed Father Francis, the abbey guesthouse master, to see if a room was available when she could get away. She's never met him in person—they've only communicated by e-mail and notes. He leaves her a welcoming note in her room, and she writes him a thank-you note when she leaves. She has a warm feeling towards Father Frances who, on behalf of the Benedictine monks at the abbey, always extends such hospitality to her. "All guests who present themselves are to be welcomed, for He himself will say, 'I was a stranger and you welcomed me.'" The last time Miriam was at the monastery, Father Fran had said on his welcoming note, "I'll be praying for you." That had taken her by surprise, living as she does in such a secular world. Yet during the three days she was there, she relished the thought that she was included in Father Fran's prayers. What a strange and beautiful thing!

Father Fran knows she comes to the monastery to write. To write, and also to get away from her caretaking duties. A little holiday. She was upfront about her needs when she first inquired about a room. She didn't want to use the guestrooms for something they weren't intended for, but Father Fran had no problem. She figures the other retreatants are more religious than she. They're there to study the Bible, attend services, or maybe use the library to do scholarly research. And there are those who come to pray, probably. Maybe a few come just to get away from the demands of the world.

Miriam herself likes to get away from the demands of the world, her world. For a few days, no one needs her: not Ted, not her mother, not her students, her friends. Or if they do, they can wait. For now, she is taking care of herself. Don't all the magazines recommend that? She intends to write something, she's not sure what. It's just that she feels some internal pressure hard to describe. But so far, all she has is a vague desire, a few half-baked anecdotes, a memory or two, and all the holes where the skein of memory has worn thin or disappeared altogether.

At least her mother isn't in a "holiday room" anymore. If she was, Miriam wouldn't have been able to come. During the "Unforgettable" project, residents had to move out of their own rooms at some point, so that those rooms could be carpeted and painted. "Holiday room" was the euphemism Jackson-Wilkens came up with for the temporary quarters. Some holiday! The upheaval didn't bother some residents—those who didn't know the difference. But Miriam's mother had trouble going from a private room to sharing one with a stranger. Actually, she had the perfect roommate: a totally deaf and almost blind lady who didn't say a thing, didn't hear a thing, didn't do a thing.

But Miriam's mother couldn't get over the fact that someone else was in the room. "Do you know there's somebody in that bed over there?" she had whispered to Miriam on one of her first days in the holiday room. Another time she asked anxiously, "Am I supposed to take care of her?" How to explain it all? Miriam tried, but her mother couldn't retain the information. And before too long, she was screaming in the hall. Unforgettable.

When Miriam pulls into St. John's, it is still snowing and everything is coated with a heavy blanket of white. But she feels good. St. John's is a small college campus, with the monastery set between the old church and the new church. She's arrived at a sanctuary. Getting her suitcase from the car, she's pelted by a cold, mean assault to her face, as if someone is peppering her with cold sand. Along the walk narcissus are in bloom, but weighed down to the ground. It's almost five o'clock. It's taken her longer than usual to get here, because of the snow. Dinner service begins at five-thirty. She likes the food they serve in the abbey guesthouse dining room. Catholic steam-table food, there when you go in, all set out as if by fairies, the good Catholic women working in the kitchen downstairs. *Io ho fame e io ho ...* She can't remember the word for "tired." *Fatigué?* No, that's French.

Is that what it feels like to her mother when she can't remember a word or make a sentence? As if she's trying to speak a foreign language she's just beginning to learn? How frustrating and confusing it must be for her mother, the way it is for Miriam when she knows what she wants to say in Italian, but can't remember how. Often she'll feel that what she intends to say is right there, on the tip of her tongue, but her brain can't move. Her brain actually feels stuck. Is that how her mother feels most of the time?

She checks in at the reception desk in the Great Hall,

as the old church is now called. She's delighted to see that she's gotten room 104. She always gets 104, probably because it's the guest room most often used for short-term stays. But she prefers to think it's because she's meant to have room 104, that it is *her* room, the place she belongs when she comes here.

She opens the door to that simple space: an entry hall, and then a small room with two single beds, a wooden desk with a lamp and chair, books held by granite book-ends, two sitting chairs and a floor lamp. A large picture window. Everything she could possibly need, and no more.

She goes to the window to look out. She is deeply attached to and somehow moved by this view. The monastery is set back between the old church, a Romanesque-style edifice of red bricks, handmade and fired at the abbey in the 1860s, and the massive modern concrete and steel church, designed by Marcel Breuer. It has an imposing bell tower in front, a slab that's 112 feet high by 100 feet wide holding aloft two open windows, one with a cross and the other the bronze bells that ring every hour on the hour, plus four times a day to call the monks and community to services.

Between these two churches is the monastery courtyard, a cloistered area behind a high red brick wall, into which Miriam looks from her picture window. What appeals to her is the way she's set back from the world behind this courtyard and wall, yet she can see out, through the grid of the wrought-iron double gates, one of which is open. She can gaze upon students, college personnel, and an occasional monk, all passing by on the quadrangle between the two churches, all at a remove. There is something infinitely peaceful about being inside the courtyard, where no one ventures except an infrequent monk, crossing on the far walkway.

Adding to the sense of serenity that Miriam feels when she looks out the window are the two clumps of ancient birch trees in the courtyard, one to the left of her window, white and gray against the old red brick church, and the other to the right, framing the massive concrete wall of the modern church. Perhaps they have been here as long as the abbey itself—they look grizzled and hoary with their peeling, shredding curlicues of bark. The bark is a study in shades of gray, white, black, charcoal, silver. Miriam feels she could never tire of seeing those trees.

There is also a small cluster of what looks like dogwood trees in the courtyard, not far from her window. In South Carolina the dogwood, pink or white, bloom around Easter. Their Sunday-school teacher showed them the blossoms in the shape of the cross, with the crown of thorns in the center. These dogwood, a Northern variety, have yet to leaf out. Snow lies thick on their thin branches. And the vines that grow up the brick courtyard walls are just black, veiny lines now. Not a leaf in sight, though she can sense that the grass under the snow is ready to green up.

On the guest-room desk, Miriam finds a welcoming note from Father Francis, along with a green parking permit to put in her car. She doesn't really understand monks and nuns. They're outside her experience. But she always likes to be here, in their world for a little while. She respects their choice, to give their lives to God. "Prefer nothing whatever to Christ," St. Benedict said. There's a cross on her wall, a simple wooden one. She's grateful to imbibe the atmosphere here, of prayer, work, scholarship, and hospitality to strangers like herself. She reads the verse quoted on the little pamphlet on her desk, which lists the schedule of services and meals for retreatants: "Come by yourself to an out-of-the-way place and rest awhile."

At 5:35 she goes into the abbey guest dining hall, a cozy room with one wall of the original red brick and several long wooden tables and small wooden chairs with crosses carved into the backrests. Tonight it's pork pieces with barbeque sauce, wild rice, and green beans in mushroom sauce. There's always soup, salad in a clear glass bowl, several bottles of dressing to choose from, and a dessert of frosted cake squares or cobbler.

A group of four occupies one end of a long wooden table; the monks entertain guests in this dining room. Miriam sits by herself at the end of another table. When a woman comes in, another retreatant, she asks Miriam if she might join her. Miriam, at the risk of sounding impolite, says she isn't speaking, then quickly amends herself to say she's observing silence, which she believes is the proper, Catholic lingo. The chance to avoid conversation is one reason she comes here. She has too much racket in her head as it is. Several years ago, on her first retreat here, she made the mistake of talking in the dining room to another person who happened to be a writer. They're everywhere! Now she's learned that it's okay not to talk, but to sit and eat in silence.

Back in her room after dinner, Miriam sits in one of the chairs and looks out *la finestra*. She really was awful in Italian today. She needs to study. She brought her Italian flash cards, which she diligently makes on three-by-five cards, but never looks at. Occasionally she'll see a monk passing by in a long black robe. They seem to favor Birkenstocks, even in the snow. Is that because Christ is always pictured in sandals? It's still early, still light out, and she considers trying to write. But instead, she just sits, watching the light change to dusk.

Thursday morning. She awakes early and pulls back the heavy curtains. It's going to be a fine spring day. The sun is out, casting a daffodil light into the courtyard, where last night's snow is a fading memory. Winter is vanquished overnight, or seems so it seems. A resurrection of sorts, she can't help thinking, as the bells toll to call the monks to seven o'clock service.

After breakfast, back in her room, Miriam has the whole day before her in which to write. Only she feels the most overwhelming desire to crawl back into her little monk-like bed and sleep. Who's to know? She often feels sleepy or downright fatigued when she has to write, especially when she's about to start something new. It's like standing at the bottom of a huge mountain she'll have to climb, one step at a time, one word at a time. And just now it's so quiet, peaceful, and bright outside.

No wonder she's tired, she rationalizes. She never sits down, it seems, never has time. So now, when she actually feels her life *stop*—like a train suddenly grinding to a halt on the track, all the speed, noise, and forward motion abruptly stilled—it produces in her an eerie sense of vertigo, silence, and surprise. She lies down on top of the covers and falls into a deep, twenty-minute sleep, the kind of oblivion where your bones let go.

Back at her desk, she turns on her laptop. The thing scares her a little. She's used to her computer at home and hardly uses this portable one. It's always unfamiliar and awkward when she turns it on again after a long hiatus. There's a little knob in the middle, instead of a mouse, and for some perverse reason it always makes Miriam think of a clitoris, the way it gets manipulated in little circles by the finger. Obviously any distraction will do!

She stares at the blank screen, trying to conjure words. But when none come, she decides she'll just browse a bit in other people's words, warm up a bit, like stretching before exercise, maybe. The monks have thoughtfully provided some reading material, and she's brought a book, *Searching for Memory*, about current research on the nature of memory. She plucks a pamphlet from between the stone bookends, still sleepy, hoping one day to wake up. It's a short history of the area around St. Cloud. She reads about the Grasshopper Chapel in Cold Spring, which she's never heard of. "Built as a symbol of prayer, the chapel represents the miracle of an April 26, 1877, snowstorm that halted an impending grasshopper plague." It had not occurred to her that a late April snowstorm would ever be a miracle to anyone. Biblical images of locusts swarming, black as an approaching thunderhead, come to mind. And then the dropping temperatures, the cold white snow.

She can't resist opening the Bible. She hasn't read the Bible in years, really, but it's familiar to her, from all those days of Sunday school at Earle Street Baptist. Matthew, Mark, Luke, and John, the poetry of her childhood.

And when the Sabbath was past, Mary Magdalene, and Mary the mother of James, and Salome, had brought sweet spices, that they might come and anoint him ... And they said among themselves, Who shall roll away the stone from the door of the sepulcher? And when they looked, they saw that the stone was rolled away: for it was very great. And entering into the sepulcher, they saw a young man sitting on the right side, clothed in a long white garment; and they were affrighted. And he saith unto them, Be not affrighted: Ye seek Jesus of Nazareth, which was crucified: he is risen; he is not here. Behold the place where they laid him.

Miriam's mother thinks that her own mother, husband, and two brothers are still alive. They've risen from the dead in her mother's mind, for at one time she knew their deaths. Knew that her kid brother, Johnny, died at twenty-two when his plane was sabotaged over France in the Second World War. Knew her father dropped dead of a heart attack, two days after receiving news of Johnny's death. Knew her mother died at age ninety-two in the Oakview Nursing Home. Knew her husband, Miriam's father, died of a heart attack ten years ago. Knew, or at least was told, that her remaining brother, Elmo, died last year in a nursing home in Texas. But often, her mother will speak of her dead as if they're alive. *Let's be sure and tell Mama* (about the roses blooming in the courtyard at Jackson-Wilkens). *Have you seen your daddy lately? Call Elmo to come get me!* They live on in what people see as a broken memory. But maybe her mother's memory exists in another dimension. Maybe it's managed to shed the bonds of time.

Miriam opens *Searching for Memory* and reads, "Great is the power of memory, a fearful thing, O my God, a deep and boundless manifoldness; and this thing is the mind, and I myself." — Augustine.

Almost lunch time. Still no writing. Why is it so hard! Why can't she just, well, write? She tries a few paragraphs, but everything comes out sounding self-conscious, forced.

Dead. Whatever needs to open up in her and speak is silent.

She opens *Searching for Memory* again. In it are photographs of artworks by artists representing "memory's fragile power." One that particularly catches Miriam's eye is of an old suitcase, upright on its side and open. Her parents always packed a lot of suitcases to go on trips, filling the big trunk of their Buick, back in the Sixties. Where are all those old Samsonite suitcases now? Perhaps they're in museums, standing open on their sides. The one in the photograph is blurred in its gray and white reproduced tones. She can't quite tell, but one side looks to be covered with a chicken-wire type grid—to hold in the contents? Miriam notes those satiny, elastic straps her mother always pulled across packed clothes, neatly folded and layered with tissue paper to keep them from wrinkling. The other side looks as if it holds clouds, the sky. There's a face emerging, hard to make out. Materializing from a tear in the paper, she reads, is a ghostly, yet affecting old photograph of the artist's brother, who died at an early age.

How appropriate, she thinks, this suitcase of memory. You can unpack it at your leisure, or fold it up and take it with you, wherever you go.

Today's lunch is something she never gets at home: a big fat greasy Polish sausage, with rice and frozen vegetables. Eating in silence, Miriam thinks of the video tape she had made out of the few rolls of old home movies she kept when they sold the house in Greenville and moved her mother to Minnesota. Her father was always interested in photography and had too many carousels of slides, shoe boxes of snapshots, and rolls of old home movies for her to contend with. Many of the home movies had been ruined by heat and time, but Miriam kept the five or six that seemed salvageable and had them converted to video this past Christmas. There were her parents with Linda as a toddler, moving, talking (silently), animated in black and white. Being three years younger than Linda, it had taken Miriam a while to get into the picture, so to speak. When she did, she was lying on her stomach with black curly hair, her tongue going in and out like a lizard's.

It was her parents that amazed her—their young selves. She could hardly believe how strong and vigorous her father looked in his bathing suit, swimming in Table Rock Lake, rising up out of the water, black-haired and muscular. He had been so little for so long in old age that it was hard to believe he had ever been any other way. But there he was, unmistakable. And her mother, pleasingly plump in her bathing suit, plunging into the water. Miriam's grandmother, her mother's mother, Maud, in what could only be called a bathing costume—downright Victorian—is holding Linda in waist-deep water. Miriam's mother swims by, kicking a little water up at them, laughing in her bathing cap.

Miriam had debated showing the video to her mother. She was afraid it might confuse her more, make her believe that *then* was *now*. But of course her mother already believes that then is now, that everything is now, really. She wasn't bothered by the past brought to life in such a way. She seemed happy to see people whom she could actually recognize, as opposed to the strangers around her at Jackson-Wilkens. Watching the tape with her, Miriam had the strange sensation that she herself had been wrong about time, thinking of it as a river rushing them downstream, when it was actually a lake where they could float and swim.

• • •

After lunch, Miriam looks through some old things she brought with her in a manila envelope with the word "Mother" scrawled across it. A few of her mother's old letters, and some journal writing Miriam has done over the years about her mother. Maybe something here will spark her, inspire her. Resurrect her from the deadness of not-writing.

She opens a small notecard with a picture of a lighthouse on the front. It is dated June 20, 1995, and she recognizes her mother's handwriting. Her mother used to have excellent penmanship, but here Miriam can see that her handwriting has already become a little wobbly, the lines not straight on the unlined paper. She reads: *Dear Miriam: So glad to have your card, telling I have your visit to look forward to a nice visit with you. We will have a good time together.*

Today, I went to the McAlister Square to get fitted with new glasses. My eye Dr. had fitted me over a month ago. I got two pr. the dark and plain. Will go back next week for a fitting. I had the ones I am wearing for five years. Frances took me. We went at 9:00 a.m. and they didn't open until 10—But I got the same young man I had before and am pleased with my order. Will get them next week.

Lucille and Vim took Grace and me to the Peach orchard last Wed. so I've had some delicious peaches. We'll go again while you're here for the late ones. It's a sight to see so many.

Still watching O. J.

Love, Mother

Only five years ago her mother could write a pretty lucid letter, address it, and mail it. A widow for the previous five years, she was still living at home then, with the help of Frances three days a week, the last in the long line of black women who had made her mother's whole life possible, it seems. By the following January, it would become apparent that her mother couldn't live on her own any-more. Something catastrophic must have happened in her brain, a burst blood vessel, a stroke, as a doctor once told Miriam, deep in her brain. Or maybe many strokes. May-be it was Alzheimer's, beginning its stranglehold. They didn't really know. Whatever it was, it was what they used to call senility, though researchers now say it isn't normal, that kind of severe memory loss, even in old age. Miriam wonders if she'll "get" the same thing. Her mother, her grandmother—talk about legacies!

One day not too long ago, Miriam arrived to find her mother napping. When Miriam gently woke her, it took her mother a long time to "come to," as if she were be-ing awakened from a deep dream. She looked around and tried to place herself. "Miriam," she said, "am I going crazy? I can't remember a thing! I must be going crazy!" *Where was she? How had she come to be there? When had she arrived? What was going on?*

Miriam wheeled her into the bathroom and helped her wipe her face with a wet washcloth, hoping that would comfort and revive her. She looked with her mother at their reflections in the mirror over the sink. "You're not crazy, Mother. You know who I am. But you're old, you're ninety years old. You're not supposed to be able to re-member everything."

"I'm ninety years old?" her mother had asked, in some-thing like horror. She stared at her own face in the mirror, her hair dyed golden brown still, the way she liked it.

"You don't feel ninety, do you?" Miriam asked, and her mother shook her head, no, her expression for all the world like a young girl's. "Do you know how old I am, Mother?"

Her mother looked at Miriam's image in the mirror above her own head. "Nine," she had said at last. "Nine or ten."

• • •

Miriam decides to go out for a walk. She doesn't want to be in her cell, as she thinks of it, any longer. Why waste such a beautiful day? It's amazingly spring-like outside, and she walks around the college campus connected to the monastery, taking in the sights. She decides she much prefers the old red brick church to the huge new one with its cold concrete statement, as if it's shouting. The students are out and about, finishing lunch, changing classes, enjoying the sunshine. They all wear blue jeans and look innocent, untouched in their youth, though she knows that's not true in every case.

Miriam, in her silence and solitude, passes through them. She likes being where she is completely unknown and knows no one. She thinks of all the college students she has taught—faces, names, stories, moments come and go, not definite memories so much as impressions, a felt sense, all in a fluid jumble. There have been so many students! Once upon a time she believed that she would never forget a student—never forget a name, a face, the relevant details. It pains her to realize how much she's forgotten, or misplaced, about so many things.

She follows the road behind campus that runs alongside a lake. Lake Sagatagan, she reads on a road sign. Lakes have always figured prominently in her life. She has a book of meditations by Jon Kabat-Zinn, *Wherever You Go There You Are*, which she would cherish for the title alone. Her favorite meditation is the lake meditation, where you lie on the floor and imagine that you're a lake, reflecting everything around you. Sometimes your surface is rough and choppy, but underneath, all is calm, serene, a deep reservoir.

Her mother's room at Jackson-Wilkens looks out at Cedar Lake. Her mother, it turns out, really enjoys the view out her window. She's thrilled to see the lake every day and often exclaims about how it "comes up blue" every morning. In the winter, it "comes up white."

Miriam refers to the lake as Mr. Lake. "How's Mr. Lake today?" she asks her mother. It's an echo from a Eudora Welty story called "Moon Lake," which she read in her twenties, when she was in graduate school. She still remembers how one of the camp counselors from "up North" exhorts the Morgana girls and county orphans to wade into "Mr. Dip." That story was one of the reasons Miriam wanted to become a writer in the first place. To try to write like Eudora Welty seemed the worthiest thing she could try to do with her life. Miriam had taken the vows a long time ago.

Today, Lake Sagatagan is dark blue, cold looking, framed by bare trees on the far bank. What is the Italian word for lake? She searches her memory—she knows she's heard it recently. Nothing there, except a wisp of that song she was playing in the car yesterday. She realizes she doesn't need her coat. The day is actually warm, spring-like, and there's even an unmistakable sense of anticipation in the air that she can't explain. A gathering of internal energy, a prelude to bursting out into leaf—into song, Miriam can't help thinking.

She walks up a hill on a dirt road between two columns of leafless trees, which might be some form of poplar. They're very tall and narrow, all their strength and energy, it seems, every branch in fact, reaching upwards, upwards towards God—or at least to the sun. The trees seem to be positively standing on tiptoe to touch the sky. And they look dead. Bare and dead looking. Hard to believe they'll ever green up again. But sure enough, on close inspection, Miriam sees that they have tiny buds.

At the top of the hill is a cemetery. Miriam loves a good cemetery, and this appears to be an excellent one. For starters, it's completely deserted on this delicate spring afternoon, when the air feels newborn. This is where the monks are buried. She sees row after even row of gravestones, all uniform, dark gray granite—first names on one side (Bede, Herman, Andrew, Rupert, Placid, Ambrose, Conrad, Aloysius, Leo, Wolfgang)—and last names on the other. There are no expressions of grief or faith; just the facts. Some of the birth dates go back to the early 1800s. The monks have climbed this hill many times to bury their dead. The abbots are set apart in covered crypts, and there's a large cross at the crest of the hill. Behind the cross, down the far side, is a little river, and down the side Miriam just walked up is Lake Sagatagan.

It's peaceful on top of the little cemetery hill. Miriam feels perfectly at home here. She sits down on a wooden bench: *Come by yourself to an out-of-the-way place and rest awhile* ... Cemeteries are another of the continuous threads in her life. First, the one at Ebenezer Baptist, outside of Traveler's Rest, where her father's parents and grandparents are buried in South Carolina. From the time she can remember, her folks would put flowers on the graves there. Her grandmother, Maud, her mother's mother, always wanted to go to Lima Baptist, another cemetery on a mountain top, to visit her own mother's grave. After she got her driver's license, Miriam would drive her up there to the country. Her grandmother's mother had died in 1900, when Maud was ten years old. Miriam must be the last living person to know where her grandmother's mother is buried.

Then there's Woodlawn Memorial Cemetery, in Greenville, where her father, his brothers, her uncles H.C. and Perry, and their wives, her Aunt Alma and Aunt Grace, are all buried. It's where her mother will be buried one day. Miriam and Linda had their mother's name and birth date engraved on the joint tombstone when they buried their father. One day in the unknown future, they'll fill in the rest. Woodlawn must have been practically country when her father bought the plots, but now it's surrounded on two sides by busy highways. You can see a Midas Muffler shop and a Red Lobster Restaurant from her father's gravesite.

Her parents loved going to Red Lobster. Miriam smiles at the memory of taking them out to dinner there in their old age. Her little father, in his eighties, dressed so snappily in plaid pants, a knit shirt, and running shoes—of all things!—and her mother donned the full monty: girdle, bra, nylon undies, hose, slip, nice shoes, a pretty dress, and one of her many pocketbooks with a linen hankie, compact, and rain bonnet, just in case. Her mother no longer has any dresses in her closet. When she moved to the nursing home, they abandoned her girdles, which were too difficult to pull up and down, and gradually got rid of all her dresses. Now she wears only pants with elasticized waists and washable blouses.

Writing. What is it she wants to say? Maybe what she really wants to write is a Book of the Dead. But no one would want to read such a book. She ought to at least write something people want to read, for Pete's sake! Fiction. Made-up characters. Amazing plots, dynamic action. Mysteries and thrillers are big. How does anyone spend a year or more thinking about whether it was the candlestick in the library or the noose in the pantry? Miriam couldn't do it. Still, she admires those writers whose minds are filled with something besides their aging mothers, dead people, and a recurring song.

She gets up and walks among the tombstones, studying them, wondering about the monks who rest in peace here. What were they like, what were their choices in life, and what, in the end, did they make of it all? Who remembers them now? She's sure some of them are still remembered, loved beyond death. Others have been absorbed back into the great Forgetting of the universe.

"Live and learn, die and forget it all," her grandmother used to say. Miriam has to smile at that. Maybe that's behind Miriam's writing all these years—she's always writing everything down so she *won't* forget. She thinks of the boxes of her old journals, those from the seventies and eighties mainly, stashed up in the attic. They've been up there for years now and she never gives them a thought.

What if she forgets—Oh God!—that they're up there! She can just see herself and Ted getting older and frailer, having to sell the house, move into assisted living, then a nursing home, if they both make it that far. A young couple buys their house and one day discovers Miriam's journals in the attic and—gasp—reads them. Not that they're riveting, but still. She should make a note, have it laminated, and tack it to her study wall: *Journals in Attic! Don't forget!*

That night Miriam goes to bed early. She's tired, with the kind of fatigue that comes from wanting to do something she can't. Her head feels full, yet blocked. But Miriam's been there before. Sometimes writing has to do with waiting. Waiting can be hard work.

She dreams she's holding a final conversation with her mother. They're talking on the phone, and she realizes her mother is dying. She understands that this is the last time she'll hear her voice. Nothing can change that. Then there is another dream, in which she receives the news that her mother has died. Miriam falls over like a statue. She falls over as if she is made of stone. Face down, with nothing to break her fall.

Then she is somewhere in Italy, which she recognizes,

though she's never been there, and she's carrying a heavy suitcase. She knows the language fluently and she knows where she is going. She lugs her suitcase to the door of a bombed-out monastery. When she knocks, the door is opened by Neva, the young black woman who took care of Miriam when she was a baby. Miriam is amazed to see her, but Neva has been expecting Miriam. She shows her to her room, which has a view of a lake. She tells Miriam that prayers will be starting soon and Miriam nods her head, she understands ... There's a knock on the door. It's Father Fran, whom she recognizes, though she has never seen him before. Without speaking, he indicates that he wants to whisper something in her ear. She feels his hand cup her head gently and his words are like a blessing: *Never forget!*

Friday morning. She awakes feeling deeply rested, as if she's slept the sleep of the dead. It feels as if during the night, something has done the work she has been trying so willfully and hopelessly to force. She opens the blinds and looks out on the courtyard. Winter on Wednesday, spring on Thursday, and now, on Friday, with the bells ringing once again, it's something else—an in-between day of silvers and grays.

In her nightgown, she sits down at the desk and takes up her pen. Before her is the familiar yellow legal pad. It doesn't seem so hard, really—writing. It is hard, she knows, but she feels herself step aside, bow out. A lot of *shoulds* fly out of her head, leaving only desire and necessity.

Without stopping to think, she begins to write. She describes how, when she stopped by her mother's room on Wednesday, her mother wasn't there. She was at the beauty parlor down the hall, as Miriam knew she would be. Miriam put away clean underwear in her mother's chest of drawers. Even though she was in a hurry to get on the road, to drive to the monastery, she took a moment to look out the window at Mr. Lake. Then she walked down the hall and around the corner to the beauty shop, to find her mother.

Writing, she passes the newly painted murals on the corridor's walls, compliments of the "Unforgettable" campaign—flowers spilling over fences and climbing up trellises, windows opening to blue skies and clouds, birds flying, butterflies landing—to the beauty parlor's door. She stops at the threshold and looks inside. There is her mother, her hair in curlers, asleep under a dryer. Miriam pauses for what seems an eternal moment, looking at her mother's face, memorizing it. Then she crosses to her mother, stoops down beside her wheelchair, and places her hand on her mother's bare, cool, incredibly soft arm. Her mother opens her eyes and looks right at Miriam, confused. Then the light of recognition floods her face and she grasps Miriam's hand. Miriam feels an electric current run through her, the warm urgency of her mother's life ...

Writing is her religion, her resurrection. Long after her mother is gone, she will have this moment. Her mother will rise from the dead and live again in those words, grasping Miriam's hand in her own. Miriam understands what she must do. She will write her stories, she will pack a suitcase, she will travel to a foreign place where she knows the language, the language of loss. And she will sing.

Acknowledgments

Love and gratitude to my sister, Betty Bates, who traveled the long road with me.

Special thanks to Phyllis Bellin, and to Jones-Harrison Residence in Minneapolis, for the kind, professional care my mother received in the last years of her life.

Thanks to Todd Maitland, Editor, and David Unowsky, Publisher, of *Ruminator Review*, for publishing "Lost Lake."

Thanks to The Minnesota Center for Book Arts, for commissioning "Swimming, Snow" as their 1993 Winter Book. It was an incredible honor to have my story produced by so many amazing book artists.

Thanks to James Ashley Shea, Margaret Diehl, and Ingrid Case for copyediting help.

Thanks to Louise Roche for her incredible proofreading. Any further mistakes are all mine!

Judy Liautaud, enormous gratitude for the simple, perfect cover design, and for struggling through purple, mud, and turquoise proofs with me to arrive at the true blue sky I wanted.

Thanks to Rob, Amy, and Sarah at 52novels.com for their usual great ebook and print-on-demand formatting.

Heartfelt thanks to all of you who've let me know that you enjoy and appreciate my writing. It means a lot.

Jeff, husband and editor extraordinaire, what can I say (yet again)? I couldn't do any of it—the life or the writing–without you. Profound love and thanks.

About the Author

Paulette Alden is the author of *Feeding the Eagles*, an earlier collection of Miriam Batson short stories; *Crossing the Moon*, a memoir; and the novel *The Answer to Your Question*, which won The Kindle Book Review's 2013 Best Indie Book Award in the suspense category. A former Stegner Fellow and Jones Lecturer in Creative Writing at Stanford, Alden has taught memoir and fiction writing extensively, at the University of Minnesota, Carleton College, St. Olaf College, and the Key West Literary Seminar. Originally from South Carolina, Alden lives in Minneapolis, where she critiques manuscripts and blogs on books and writing on her website, www. paulettealden.com.

If you enjoyed UNFORGETTABLE, it would be a great help if you would post a review of it on Amazon and/or Goodreads and let other readers know why you liked it. Thanks so much!

Paulette Alden is available for readings and book groups. Please contact her via her website, www.paulettealden. com